WIND WARRIOR

Jon Messenger

Clean Teen Publishing
PO Box 561326
The Colony, TX 75056

http://www.cleanteenpublishing.com

Content Discolsure

For more information about our content disclosure, please utilize the QR code above with your smart phone or visit us at www.CleanTeenPublishing.com.

To Jacki and Alistair
Who showed me that only by combining brains and
beauty can you hope to change the world.

THE EARTH GIVES WAY TO THE SEA,
THE SEA BOWS BEFORE THE WIND,
THE WIND FEEDS THE FLAME,
THE FLAME BURNS THE WORLD OF MAN
DOWN TO THE EARTH.

CHAPTER 1

Xander Sirocco leaned back in his seat at the back of the White Halls College lecture hall. Reaching up, he rubbed his eyes as the professor droned on in the front of the class. His hands slid down from his eyes and covered his mouth just in time to suppress a strong yawn.

Brushing his dark hair out of his eyes, Xander looked down at his thick notebook sitting on the flip-out tabletop in front of him. His copious notes were intermixed with doodles of dragons, giants, and cartoonish characters in various stages of murdering one another.

"That's cute," Jessica said from beside him as she leaned over and looked at his drawings. She pointed to a silhouetted figured with a gaping hole in his chest and a cannon ball sitting on the ground behind him. "That one's my favorite."

Xander looked over at the sorority girl and flashed her a smile. "It's how I felt about halfway through this class."

The blonde girl covered her mouth as she laughed, trying not to let the professor hear the disruption. Though the lecture hall was built like stadium seats and large enough to hold over a hundred students, most classes at White Halls contained barely over twenty.

As the professor continued lecturing, Jessica leaned over again and whispered into his ear. "Are you going to the spring formal next weekend?"

Xander shrugged. The spring formal was one of the largest events on campus and everyone he knew would be attending. Unfortunately, his grades had been slipping recently and he knew what his parents would say—grades came first. Of course, he knew his grades wouldn't be suffering if he started paying more attention in class and spent less time doodling.

"I'll try, but I can't make any promises."

Jessica pouted and Xander knew his resolve would quickly weaken. He and Jessica had known each other since sharing classes their freshman year. Though they weren't officially dating, they spent quite a bit of time together and he was sure she wouldn't be resistant if he expressed interest.

"I'll try," he reiterated.

"That's good enough… for now," she replied impishly.

Jessica's expression suddenly changed and she furrowed her brow as goose bumps erupted across her skin. She crossed her arms over her chest and rubbed her exposed skin, trying to warm up.

"Did they just turn on the air conditioning?" she complained. "It's suddenly freezing."

Xander held out his hand but didn't notice a draft or breeze. "Do you want my jacket?"

Jessica nodded and Xander retrieved his pea coat

from the seat beside him. She threw it over her upper body and snuggled against the thick jacket.

"You sure you're not just having menopausal hot flashes?" Xander joked to the nineteen-year-old.

Jessica pursed her lips and elbowed him in the ribs. They were both still laughing as the professor concluded his lecture.

"Don't forget to read chapters sixteen through twenty before next week's class," the professor said as the class stood and collected their bags.

Xander took his time putting his books and pens back into his backpack. Jessica stood beside him and stretched. Surprisingly, she handed him back his jacket.

"Feeling better?" he asked.

"Yeah," she said with a slow nod. "It's strange but I don't feel cold anymore."

"Hot flashes. Told you so."

She laughed as she threatened to hit him again. "You're such a jerk."

Xander followed her into the corridor and out the back doors of the lecture hall. The room emptied into the building's foyer and the three sets of double doors that exited onto the aptly named College Street.

The pair merged with the rest of the exiting students and walked down the wide stairs.

"Think about the formal," Jessica said. "You really should come."

"I have to run it by my family first." He held up a hand before she could make a snide remark. "I know— I'm twenty and I live with my parents."

"And your grandfather," she quickly added.

Xander frowned playfully. "Yes, thank you for that reminder. But they're paying for college and I still have obligations to them. If I can make it—"

"You better."

"*If* I can make it," he said again, "I promise I'll let you know."

A gentle wind kicked up from behind them as they reached the street. It blew across Xander's back as they walked and sent his dark hair cascading down his forehead and into his eyes, leaving him little visibility beyond the next few squares of weathered sidewalk. He absently brushed his hair aside but a sudden gust of frigid wind threw his hair back into his face.

"Man, it's freezing around here," Jessica said. "I thought it was supposed to warm up in April?"

"No one told Mother Nature, apparently."

"Mother Nature is being a jerk," she joked. "Which way are you heading?"

Xander pointed across the street. "I parked in the gravel lot."

He rubbed a hand over the two days of stubble that coated his cheeks as another cool breeze blew across him. Despite the chill he felt on the end of his nose and the threatening cold it foretold, he was glad for the warmth his scraggly beard provided. The unseasonably cool weather left him shivering and wishing that the White Halls College had parking closer to campus. The walk from his lecture hall to the parking lot was only a few blocks but the wind was strong enough to gust aside the tails of his pea coat. Xander pulled the front of his jacket closed as he and Jessica stopped at the crosswalk.

"I have to head back to the Tri Delta house," she said, motioning the opposite direction from where he was heading. "I'm serious. Think about the formal."

"Hey Xander," a heavyset student said, pushing his way up beside the pair.

"Hi Sean," Jessica said flatly as she looked at the man with disdain.

Sean wore a big smile, which matched the large Captain America T-shirt he wore proudly beneath his thin windbreaker. Xander found the smile infectious and, despite the cold, found himself smiling in return.

"How's it going, Sean?" he asked.

Sean shrugged. "I didn't think I'd catch you when you came out of class. I had to run the whole way here."

"Color me impressed," Jessica said sarcastically.

Xander shot her a sour look but let the smile return before he looked back at Sean.

"I'm glad you did. You park in the gravel lot?"

Jessica placed a hand on Xander's arm, getting his attention. "I'm going to go ahead and take off. Call me and let me know if you can go."

She leaned over and kissed him on the cheek. With a light wave, she turned and walked away.

"Go where?" Sean asked.

Xander sighed as he watched her walk away. "She wants me to go to the formal with her."

"Is it possible for you two to go together and not have her talk all night? She's hot, but really annoying."

Xander laughed despite immediately feeling guilty. "You be nice too. Anyway, anything new with you?"

Sean stroked his chin. "I'm still struggling with

my freshman fifteen three years later, so no, not really."

Xander laughed again. Sean and Xander looked odd, standing side by side. Xander had been blessed with good metabolism and had always been athletic. No matter the horrible college food he ate—and he had eaten his fair share of pizza and microwave macaroni and cheese—he stayed thin. Sean, however, wasn't nearly as lucky. He'd been struggling with his weight since they met in middle school but college seemed to give him a chance to stop worrying about impressing people and be happy. It was food that made Sean happy.

"How are your folks?" Sean asked.

"Folk-y," Xander replied with a shrug. "It's hard enough to be in college without having to live with your parents. I'm pretty sure I'm drifting further and further away from 'cool'."

"Don't forget your grandfather lives there too," Sean chided.

"Thanks," Xander said flatly.

Sean beamed another smile. "No problem. You doing anything fun this weekend? If not, come over to the apartment."

"I don't know if I'll be able to fit it in. I've got Yahtzee with the family, and then I might mix it up and try a game of—"

Xander stopped in midsentence as a man rudely pushed his way past, talking loudly on his cell phone. As the man pushed past, he knocked Xander's backpack free from his shoulder. The swinging weight of the book-laden bag nearly knocked him from his feet.

"Excuse you!" Xander said as he righted himself.

The man ignored Xander and kept pushing his way toward the front of the throng of students. The front students parted as the man approached, cued into his presence by the grumbling of all the other students behind them.

"What a jerk," Sean grumbled.

"Yeah," Xander replied.

He watched the man reach the edge of the curb and step out into the street, despite the light still glaring an angry red "Don't Walk" hand. Xander quickly glanced down the street and his eyes widened in surprise as he saw one of the city buses hurtling toward the intersection.

"Watch out!" Xander yelled but the man didn't hear him.

The man stepped into the street, oblivious to the danger. The bus driver saw the suited man and stepped on the brakes. The tires on the bus locked and screeched loudly but the momentum drove it forward. It wasn't going to be able to stop in time to avoid hitting the man.

Xander heard a whisper in the air, a haunting melody that seemed to speak to him. The gentle breeze around him grew stronger as the wind seemed to pass through his body. In an instant, he felt an incredible surge pour through him, roaring from his abdomen to his extremities. The wind around him seemed to respond to the surge and his hair whipped chaotically as he stood in the center of the maelstrom. Involuntarily, he threw up his hands and the surge of energy rushed from him in a violent gust of wind that ripped through the crowd. The funnel of wind roared through the students and into the street, just as the bus collided with the man on his phone.

The man was thrown from his feet and crashed onto the street, his cell phone shattering as it skidded into the intersection. The bus came to a sudden stop with a hiss of decompressing air brakes. For a moment, everyone stared in stunned disbelief until finally the first of the girls in the front of the crowd screamed.

Some of the students rushed to help the collapsed man as the bus driver opened the door and hurried down the bus' steps.

"Oh my God," the bus driver moaned as he rushed to the man's side. "He stepped right out in front of me. There wasn't anything I could do! Is he—?"

"He's okay," someone said with obvious surprise.

In the center of the encircled students, the man stood up and brushed off the grime that had collected on his suit.

"There's not a scratch on you," one of the sorority sisters said. "How is that possible?"

"I didn't even feel a thing," the man said, stupefied. "It was like I was hit with a pillow. That's it!"

Sean and Xander stared in disbelief. Xander's hands shook as he lowered his arms and the strong wind suddenly died away. He felt drained, as though he just spent hours in the gym.

"That was awesome," Sean gushed. "Did you see that?"

Xander nodded weakly and pulled his pea coat tighter around his body.

"You feeling okay?"

"Yeah, just suddenly tired."

Sean pointed at the crosswalk light, which

suddenly glowed with a bright white "Walk" symbol. "The guy looks fine. Let's get out of here."

They walked in silence down College Street, stepping gingerly over the uneven pavement. They rode the crests and falls of the cracked sidewalk like the cars of a rollercoaster.

When they were out of earshot, Sean laughed with nervous excitement. "That was so cool, man. He just walked away after getting hit by a bus. He should have been flattened!"

Xander looked over his shoulder to make sure no one could hear their conversation.

"I think I—" he began before deciding better.

"You what?" Sean asked.

Xander shook his head. "You know what, it's crazy. Never mind."

"Consider it never minded."

They strolled into the gravel parking lot and weaved through the lines of cars until they reached their equally pathetic vehicles.

"You still want to come over this weekend?" Sean asked.

"Yeah, sure," Xander said distractedly.

"Awesome. Take care. I'll see you then."

Xander waved as Sean climbed into his car and drove off. The smile hung on his face until he slid behind the wheel of his car. For a long moment, Xander just held on tightly to the steering wheel until his knuckles turned white. His heart thundered in his chest and a cold sweat broke out on his brow. He couldn't remember the last time he'd felt so scared. He bounced his knee nervously as he thought about the strange sensation of the wind pouring through his body. He had trouble believing he had been responsible for saving that man's life, but he couldn't explain the surge of power he felt or the crazy winds that suddenly sprang up.

He slapped the steering wheel angrily, wiping away his crazy thoughts. "It couldn't have been me," he muttered.

Turning the key, his car started with a loud cough of black smoke out of the exhaust pipe. Dropping it into drive, he pulled out of the parking lot and turned toward his parent's house.

CHAPTER 2

Xander opened the front door to the house and hurried inside, hoping to avoid running into his family. He tossed his jacket onto the coat rack and shouldered his bag as he walked toward the stairs. As his foot struck the first step, he heard the creak of the hardwood floors behind him.

"Welcome home," his mother said. "Did you have a good day at school?"

"It was school," Xander shrugged. "It's pretty boring. I've got a lot to do so I'm probably just going to go upstairs and get caught up on some homework."

"Are you feeling okay? You're acting a little squirrely."

Xander arched an eyebrow in surprise. "No, I'm fine. Why would you say that?"

His mother placed her hands on her hips defiantly. "You just told me you're going upstairs at four in the afternoon to catch up on homework. You haven't been that devoted to homework since you were in grade school. What's going on?"

"Nothing," Xander sighed. "Does something have to be going on for me to want to do the right thing and catch up on homework?"

"I guess not," she replied in a voice that clearly showed she didn't believe him.

His mother walked over, placed her hand on his, and gave him an affectionate squeeze. "All right. You go have fun upstairs. Dinner will be ready in an hour and a half."

"Thanks, Mom," Xander said as he leaned over and kissed her on the cheek.

As she started walking toward the kitchen, Xander took the opportunity to start rushing upstairs.

"Don't forget to say hi to your grandfather," his mother called after him before he could escape.

Xander froze, his foot hovering over the top step. With a groan, he spun in place, started stomping back down the stairs, and walked into the living room. The sound of Jeopardy blared on the television, far louder than what should have been healthy for anyone sitting in the assorted chairs.

The high-backed recliner was turned away from Xander as he approached. He could see the small tuffs of his grandfather's white hair sticking up over the back of the chair and a soothing rhythm of deep breathing let him know that his grandfather had fallen asleep again watching TV. Xander looked up at the screen as they asked one of the questions in Double Jeopardy.

"What is the Battle of Chickamauga," Xander said softly, seconds before the first contestant buzzed in with the answer.

"See, I knew you were smarter than you let on," his grandfather muttered from his seat.

Xander jumped, caught unaware that the elder

man was even awake. "God, Grandpa! I thought you were asleep."

"I was, but I still heard you coming."

Xander smiled and walked around to the side of the chair. "You're so weird. You know that, don't you?"

His grandfather arched his head up to meet Xander's gaze. "At least now you know where you get it from."

Xander smiled at the old man. Though he loved his parents, he had always shared a very special connection with his grandfather. Despite the man's advanced years, his mind was incredibly sharp and he was surprisingly spry. When he wasn't napping, Xander realized with a smirk.

"Did your mom send you in here to check on me?" his grandfather asked.

"Not to check on you. Just to make sure I told you hello before I went upstairs."

"She can church it up however she likes, but she still wanted you to make sure I hadn't croaked while watching Jeopardy."

Xander laughed at the old man. He wasn't entirely sure where his grandfather had grown up but he had a litany of odd sayings that kept conversation entertaining.

"So what are you up to?" the elder man asked.

"I was going to go upstairs and work on homework," Xander lied again.

"Rubbish. That's the worst excuse I've ever heard. If you were going to work on homework, you should have just stayed at school. Or at least found a pretty girl to tutor in a class, if you get my drift."

"I get the drift, Grandpa. You're a dirty old man."

His grandfather laughed. The sound reminded Xander of an odd mix of mirth and a hacking cough.

"I'm going to head upstairs." Xander kissed the man on the top of his head before turning toward the stairs.

"Be careful up there," his grandfather said cryptically.

Xander turned to ask him what he meant, but he could already hear the repetitive breathing as his grandfather fell back asleep.

He stood in the middle of his room and stared at the bed and the plethora of posters that littered the walls. As much as he wished it weren't true, Xander still slept in the same room he grew up in and many of the decorations hadn't changed since his days of listening to hardcore rap.

His covers were bunched into a ball in the middle of the bed and dirty laundry was piled just beyond the footboard. The rest of the room was fairly clean, though Xander realized that was as much by accident as by design. Only his working table was cluttered with piles of artist's sketchpads and loose-leaf paper. His hastily drawn charcoal sketches covered all the exposed surfaces. Women's faces were piled besides blueprints for space ships. Fantasy creatures growled angrily at cartoon characters, either hand drawn or traced from Disney cells. Though Xander prided himself on his artistic ability, he wasn't foolish enough to believe he was good enough to make it more than a hobby.

Scanning the room, his eyes fell on one of the larger posters dominating the middle of the wall above the headboard. Xander flexed his shoulders and waved his arms across his body as he stretched in anticipation.

His heart was already pounding in his chest again. His hands were closed in tight fists and he could feel the intermixed sweatiness and pain as he dug his nails into his palms.

"All right," he whispered into the quiet room. "You can do this."

He focused all his attention on the poster and tried to imagine the swell of power flooding his body as it had done in front of the school. His skin grew cold and clammy, but he wasn't sure if it was from an unknown power or just the adrenaline he was intentionally pouring into his system.

"I can do this. Ready, go!"

He extended his arms and opened his hands, throwing his fingers out wide. His eyes closed involuntarily as he anticipated the violent windstorm. Slowly, he cracked one eye open and peeked at the poster. It hung unfettered on the wall, the rap trio still staring angrily at the awkward white man standing in the middle of the room with his arms outstretched.

With a huff, Xander dropped his arms. His eager anticipation turned to disappointment. The disappointment, however, was short-lived. Instead, Xander found himself fairly relieved. Whatever happened on College Street, it was just a coincidence that he witnessed that man survive what should have been a horrible car accident.

Smiling, he turned away from the poster when a swift draft flew past him. Behind him, he heard the flutter as the unpinned corner of the poster was caught up in the swirling breeze.

Xander froze. Slowly he turned, first toward his window, sure that it had been left open. When he realized it was closed, he turned instead toward the poster.

The wind was gone and the corner of the poster floated gently back into place against the wall.

"Did I just do that?" he whispered for fear of disrupting the sacred feeling in the room.

In response, a soft breeze swirled around his legs. The sheets that had unfurled from the ball of covers on his bed swayed from side to side.

Xander swallowed hard and wiped away the beading sweat forming at his hairline. He tried taking a deep breath but his mouth quivered as he tried to inhale.

"Okay."

Reaching up, he ran his hands over both sides of his face, as though it might help him wake up from what was clearly a dream.

"Okay, okay, okay, okay," he repeated like a mantra into the empty room. "Let's... let's try this again."

Xander focused on the poster. Instead of straining as hard as he had during his first attempt, he relaxed. If there was some other presence in the room with him— he was loathe to use the word 'ghost'—then it would act without his prompting.

A soft whisper of wind caught his attention seconds before the edge of the poster began to dance in the breeze. Xander couldn't decide if he should be smiling with excitement or screaming in fear. He settled on a nervous laugh that sounded like he was suffering from a horrible case of hiccups.

"More," he said and the wind responded.

The posters beside the large one began to flutter as the breeze spread across the wall. The centermost poster, with its three rappers staring angrily ahead, flapped as the wind intensified. Xander heard the screech as the tape holding the poster to the wall tore free. The poster hung precariously to the two strips of tape on the top of it before they gave way as well. The poster shot to the ceiling, caught up in a miniature cyclone.

As quickly as it appeared, the wind died away. The poster floated back down to the floor, settling on the carpet at Xander's feet.

Looking around, he took in the full destructive power of the wind that had materialized in his otherwise secluded room. His stacks of drawings had inadvertently been blown aside and were now strewn across the bed's nightstand and onto the floor. A few of the other posters drooped from where their topmost tape had pulled free from the wall. They hung over each other like victims. With a soft tearing noise, another poster pulled free and fell onto his bed.

A knock on the door scared Xander horribly and he let out a stifled scream. Clutching his chest, he turned toward the bedroom door.

"Who is it?" he asked breathlessly.

"Grandpa. Everything okay in there?"

"Yeah, Grandpa. Everything's good."

"Then open the door, idiot!"

Xander turned the handle and found his grandfather standing impatiently in the doorframe. His grandfather looked past him at the destruction in the room beyond.

"Working on homework, huh? You live in squalor."

"What do you need, Grandpa?" Xander asked patiently.

"Dinner's ready. Come on downstairs."

The rest of the family was already seated by the time he and his grandfather joined them in the dining room. Xander took his seat and ran a hand through his hair. It was tangled from the wind and slightly matted from his sweat but it didn't bother him.

His parents had already put food on the individual plates and his father stuffed pieces of a dinner roll into his mouth without looking up. Looking at his father was like looking in a slightly aged mirror. His dark hair and equally dark eyes came from his paternal side. Xander had to assume that when his grandfather was younger, he would have shared the similar features of his son and grandson.

When his father finally did look up from his dinner, his expression was piercing and sour. His gaze passed quickly over Xander before settling onto his grandfather. The two elders shared a look that left Xander feeling uncomfortable.

"What would you like to drink?" his mother

asked suddenly, pushing away from the table.

Xander broke his gaze away from the angry men and looked sympathetically to his mother. "How about a beer?"

"How about water," she said matter-of-factly.

He smiled sheepishly. "Water's fine, Mom. Thanks."

As his gaze fell back to the two men, he found their irritated gaze broken and both men eating noisily. They seemed to purposely avoid each other's occasional looks.

Xander tried to ignore his gnawing curiosity and began eating forkfuls of mashed potatoes. Before he could finish the small pile of potatoes, however, his father dropped his roll noisily onto his plate and leaned back in his chair.

"What are you going to do with your life?" he asked, staring intently at Xander.

Xander swallowed his mouthful of food and wiped the corners of his mouth with his napkin. "I'm going to college so I *can* do something with my life."

His father snorted derisively. "That's not a real college. It's where people go when they don't apply themselves enough to get into any decent schools. You're not trying on any of your assignments. You're coasting through with a 'C' average. You're a junior, for God's sake, and you've changed your major more times than your underwear."

"Where did this suddenly come from?" Xander asked, perturbed.

"Does anyone want any more to drink?" his

mother asked, trying to redirect an uncomfortable conversation.

"Stay out of this, Lily," his father interjected. "This is something he needs to hear."

"What more do you want from me?" Xander said. "I'm going to college so I don't have to work some crappy menial job like you do every day!"

"You watch your tone. Don't think I haven't noticed that you'd rather spend time with that sorority girlfriend of yours than focus on your schoolwork. Even Sean is living on his own and you're still living with your parents. When are you going to grow up?"

"Leave him alone, Jack," his grandfather said as he threw his napkin onto the table. "You need to tell him what's really upsetting you."

His father coughed once before scowling at the older man. "No, we don't."

"He has a right to know—"

"No," his father said adamantly.

"It's going to have to happen sooner rather than—"

"I said no!" his father demanded, slamming his hand down on the table. The bowls and glasses rattled from the impact.

"Is there something going on between the two of you?" Xander asked. "Something I need to know?"

"Yes," his grandfather said immediately.

"No," his father quickly corrected.

"Okay," Xander said slowly. "Is this something you'd like to share?"

"Yes," his grandfather added emphatically.

"No," his father said.

"Well, at least dinner isn't awkward or anything," Xander said.

His father grew disturbingly calm and set his fork down next to his plate. "Then you're excused."

"Excuse me?"

"Take your plate with you and go upstairs to your room."

"You're sending me to my room? You know I'm twenty, right?"

"Go to your room and let your grandfather and me talk in private," his father said sternly.

Xander sensed the danger in pushing his father further. In a huff, he pushed back his chair and grabbed his plate before walking out of the room. As he reached the stairs, he could hear the two men arguing in hushed tones.

～～

Lying back on his bed, Xander tossed a softball into the air. He deftly caught it as it fell before shifting its weight in his hand. Scowling, he threw it back into the air with enough force that it struck the ceiling with a loud thud. Xander caught it again as it fell before tossing it angrily toward the corner of his room.

A soft knock on his door startled Xander. He propped himself up on an elbow and stared at the closed door.

"Who is it?" he asked, dreading the possible answer.

"It's your mother. Can you open the door, please?"

Xander sighed and slid his legs over the side of

the bed. He strode across the room and unlocked the door. Without bothering to open it for her, he stormed back to his bad and laid back down.

His mother opened the door softly and stepped into the room.

"How are you doing?" she asked.

"I'm fine," he replied sarcastically. "Dad sent me to my room like I was a child. He does know I'm twenty, right? He does know that I'm going to graduate from college soon, right?"

His mother stood stoically, her hands crossed in front of her lap. She listened to him complain, nodding appropriately as he spoke.

"I can't wait to move out," he continued. "Get my own place and not have to put up with him anymore."

"Don't be too hard on your father," she offered. "He really does have your best interests at heart."

Xander turned sharply toward his mother. He knew his anger was misdirected but he felt it was necessary to stop her before she continued.

"Don't do that, Mom," he said flatly. "You don't have to play mediator between me and him every time he decides to be a jerk."

She walked over and patted his legs, encouraging him to move over on the bed. Xander swung his legs over the side and scooted toward the headboard, giving space for his mother to sit beside him.

"Your father can come across a little rough around the edges—"

Xander huffed at the understatement.

"—but he means well," she continued as though

oblivious to his derision. "You may not fully understand it or even appreciate it right now but he really does have your best interest at heart. He's just trying to protect you."

"He treats me like a child."

His mother smiled and placed her hand on his. "That's only because you're our child."

Xander couldn't suppress his smile. "You're so corny. You know that, right?"

"That's exactly why you love me," she said, leaning over to kiss him on the cheek. "Now forgive your father so I don't have to listen to the two of you ruin another dinner."

"That's the ulterior motive for this entire conversation?" Xander joked, feeling his frustration bleeding away. "You just wanted a civil dinner conversation?"

His mother shrugged. "I'm pretty simple like that."

She stood and walked toward the bedroom door. "Get some sleep tonight, dear."

Xander found himself smiling at the diminutive woman. She seemed such a gentle counterpoint to his father's abrasiveness. "Goodnight, Mom."

She pulled the door closed softly behind her as she left. Xander collapsed back onto the bed and stared up at the ceiling.

The next morning, Xander grabbed his backpack and cursed again at the time on the clock. He didn't intend to oversleep but he felt ridiculously drained after the excitement of the day before. Hopping on one foot, he pulled on his second shoe. The loaded backpack threatened to pull him over and he had to cling to his drawing table to keep from collapsing onto his bedroom floor.

He threw open the door and rushed down the stairs, his tennis shoes slapping loudly against the wooden staircase. He wasn't too worried about making a lot of noise, since both his mother and father had already left for work. Only his grandfather would still be home but he was usually in bed until late morning.

As he reached the foyer, Xander had to slide to a halt as his grandfather stepped around the corner from the living room. Xander clutched his chest again, growing steadily more angry at the series of surprises that seemed to encompass his life over the past couple days.

"You scared me half to death," Xander huffed.

"We need to talk," his grandfather said, ignoring Xander's irritation.

"I can't right now, Grandpa. I'm already running late for class."

Xander stepped gracefully around the old man and reached out for the door. "Maybe we can talk when I get back tonight."

"It's…" his grandfather began before sighing heavily. "Fine. Go. Just promise me you'll be careful today."

Xander smiled, though he was genuinely confused by the conversation. "I'm careful every day, Grandpa."

With a quick wave, Xander opened the door and rushed out to his car.

CHAPTER 3

"**S**ean!" Xander yelled over the crowd crossing the street.

Sean stopped, turned at the sound of his name, and waved as he caught Xander's eye. Xander ran up breathlessly and had to lean over to catch his breath before he could speak.

"What's going on, Xander?"

Xander raised his pointer finger, asking for a moment. He had run nearly the entire way from the parking lot after noticing Sean's car already there when he arrived.

"Today, after school. What do you have going on?" Xander said when he had caught his breath.

Sean shrugged. "Not a whole lot. Why?"

Xander smiled at his friend. He placed a hand on Sean's shoulder and squeezed. "I've got something you're going to need to see. Meet me after class."

He rushed off so that he wouldn't be late to class, leaving Sean standing perplexed on the sidewalk.

By the time Xander made it inside the lecture hall, most of the rest of the students were already seated. Jessica was sitting near the front with some of her sorority sisters. Xander waved when he caught her eye, but he chose to take his normal seat in the back of the room.

As he slid into the aisle, he noticed that a woman was already sitting in his seat. He didn't recognize her, which was odd in such a small class. Her blonde hair fell over her face, leaving only a faint view of her button nose beneath the loose strands of hair. As she looked over her textbook, she reached up and pushed her hair back behind her ear. With her hair brushed aside, she noticed Xander watching her from a few seats away. She looked up from her book, her pale blue eyes sparkling in the dim lecture hall lighting. She flashed a full smile at his gawking expression.

"I'm sorry," he said as he started to slide back out of the row.

"Don't be silly," she said, her voice an angelic whisper. "There's plenty of space in the row. Pull up a seat."

Xander felt suddenly self-aware as he took a seat beside her. He couldn't tell one specific feature about her that struck him as insanely beautiful but he found her completely irresistible.

"Hi," she said, flashing her entrancing smile again. She extended her hand. "I'm Sammy."

"Xander," he said as he took her hand. "Your hand is really warm."

Sammy's mouth froze in midsentence but, to her credit, she didn't withdraw her hand.

Xander blushed furiously. "That was perhaps the single most awkward thing I could have said. I might as well have followed it up with 'it puts the lotion in the basket'—"

"—or it gets the hose," Sammy finished with a laugh. "Yes, that would have made it much more awkward."

Xander laughed with her before realizing he still had her hand. He let it go and dropped his hands to his lap.

"Do I know you?" Xander said, trying to casually change the subject. "I haven't seen you in here before but you seem so familiar."

"I just transferred here. I was lucky enough to be let in after the semester started."

"That's got to be rough," he said, trying to shake the feeling that they'd met somewhere before. "Don't you have a lot of catching up to do?"

Sammy nodded. "I do, which is probably why we should listen to the professor."

Xander turned toward the front of the room and saw the professor halfway through his first slide. He reached into his bag and pulled out his books hurriedly. As he did, he saw Jessica staring at him disapprovingly from the front of the room. Xander shrugged sheepishly as he set his books on the table in front of him.

By the time the professor was on the third slide, Sammy leaned over to him. "Is this class always this boring?"

Xander hid his smile. "I wouldn't know. I'm usually asleep or doodling by this point in the class."

"Oh, lucky me, I chose the brainy type. So, show me these doodles of yours."

Keeping his eyes firmly fixed on the professor,

Xander flipped back a couple pages in his notebook until he revealed a sketch he had done of Jessica's profile.

"You're not half bad," Sammy whispered appreciatively. "I mean, you're not half good either."

"Way to endear yourself, new kid," he joked.

As he flipped back to today's page and began taking notes on the lecture, Sammy reached over and doodled on the corners of his paper. Her drawings were atrocious, but he let her draw for a few seconds before playfully swatting at her hand. They laughed before receiving a stern look from the professor. They both cleared their throats before another small chuckle escaped.

By the time class was over, Xander couldn't recall a single important thing the professor had taught that day. He and Sammy stuffed their books into their bags and stood. As he turned toward the end of the row, she pushed him playfully from behind and he nearly stumbled into Jessica, who waited impatiently at the end of it.

"Hi, Jessica," Xander said, oblivious to the obvious danger promised in her stern look. "I'd like you to meet Sammy."

Sammy waved but tried to avoid direct eye contact.

"Hi," Jessica said sweetly before taking Xander's arm. "Have you thought anymore about taking me to the formal?"

Xander felt himself being pulled away and turned apologetically to Sammy. Sammy jutted out her bottom lip and waved as he disappeared out the door.

When they were outside, Jessica leaned against

his shoulder. "Who is she?"

"Sammy? She's a new student, just transferred here."

"She transferred to White Halls College? Who does that?"

Xander shrugged. He hadn't given it much thought while they were talking—or flirting, as Xander allowed himself to realize—but it did seem a little odd.

"So what did you guys talk about?" Jessica asked. Xander could feel himself slipping into an inescapable bottomless pit in the conversation.

"Nothing important, really," he answered honestly.

"You guys sure talked about nothing for a long time."

Xander swallowed hard. As much as Jessica truly was a sweet girl at heart, she was also president of the campus' largest sorority. Every now and then, the sorority sister in her emerged and she became someone Xander didn't like. As much as she frustrated him when she was acting jealous and possessive, he wasn't in the mood to be confrontational.

He looked away from Jessica and was relieved when he saw a familiar face pushing his way through the crowd. Without answering Jessica, he raised his hand to get Sean's attention.

"Sorry, Jess. I promised Sean that we'd get together after class."

Jessica sighed. "You know the formal is in eight days, right? You're not the only person interested in taking me to the dance but you're the one I want to go with. Still, you need to make up your mind sooner rather than later if you want to go with me."

"I will," he said, dismissing Jessica as he turned toward Sean. "I'll talk to you later, okay?"

Jessica placed her hands on her hips and pursed her lips. When she realized she was going to be ignored, she threw her hands up in the air and walked away from the two boys.

"Thank you for the save," Xander said.

"What was that about? She looked like she was going to bite your head off. Did you finally realize Jessica's a black widow?"

"Very funny."

"Bye Xander," Sammy said as she walked past the pair. She brushed her hair out of her face and winked at him. "See you in class next week?"

"Of course," Xander replied, his heart pounding in his chest at the sight of her.

She smiled and turned away, her fingers lacing into the straps of her backpack.

They watched her walk away in silence, neither Sean nor Xander wanting to ruin the beautiful moment.

"Um," Sean began. "Who is that? What is her current relationship status? Why does she seem to like you?"

"Her name is Sammy," Xander laughed. "She's a new student. We met in class."

"I want one."

Xander placed his hand on Sean's shoulder. "Down boy."

"Oh no. You already have your skank Jessica. You don't get two beautiful women."

"I don't *have* Sammy. She's just being friendly."

Sean whistled softly. "I wish more women were friendly with me like that."

They watched until Sammy turned the corner and walked up High Street. When she was gone, Sean turned sharply on Xander.

"Okay. What was so important that you needed to show me?"

Xander looked around at the gathering throng of students. "Not here. Is that field behind your old house still empty?"

Sean shrugged. "Pretty sure. It's a little overgrown now and probably still has a bunch of old trash in it though."

"That's perfect. Let's go there and I'll tell you all about it."

Sean hadn't exaggerated about the status of the field. Unkempt by the owners, the crab grass had grown nearly to Xander's waist. As he walked through the field, his tennis shoes kept striking rusted cans and empty bottles, which clinked as they rolled deeper into the concealing grasses.

Xander stood in the center of the field. From the periphery, standing well away near the tree line that lined the edge of the field, Sean watched Xander stretch his arms out wide. Xander closed his eyes and tilted his head backward.

"Are you ready for this?" Xander called.

"Whatever *this* is, sure, I'm ready."

Xander heard the musical whisper of the wind as it called to him. Like a snake through the safari, the wind slithered between the tall grasses, causing them to sway and dance in rhythm. The wind kicked up around him, pulling at his clothes and hair. As the wind increased, it buffeted him from side to side, nearly causing him to lose his balance.

The sensation was like magic to Xander. The energy of the wind caressed his skin like an old lover. It enveloped him where he stood and seemed to pour through his open mouth, filling him with its energy. When he was satisfied with the demonstration, he exhaled, forcing the soothing winds from his lungs.

As quickly as the wind began, it died away, leaving Xander standing alone again in the middle of the field. He lowered his arms and turned excitedly toward Sean.

"Did you see it?"

"See what?"

Xander gestured behind him, and then turned in a tight circle. "The wind."

"The wind," Sean replied flatly.

"Did you see the wind blowing through the field? That was me."

"You made a breeze? That's what you're telling me? That's what was so important? Xander, I love you like a brother, but I break wind all the time without having to drag you out to a field to see me do it."

Xander frowned at his friend's disbelief. "Fine. I was going for a small demonstration but if you want big, we'll do big."

Xander returned to the center of the field and

held his arms outstretched again. He closed his eyes but quickly opened one to peer at his friend. Sean leaned against the trunk of one of the trees, his arms crossed defensively in front of him.

"You're going to want to back up for this one."

Sean turned around and looked behind him. "I'm already at the trees. I can't go much further back."

"Get… I don't know. Get behind a tree."

"You want me to hide behind a tree while you break wind again?"

"Will you just do it?" Xander said, exasperated.

Tossing his hands in the air, Sean walked around to the backside of the tree he had been leaning against. "Is this good enough?"

"Thank you."

Xander assumed his position in the field once again, lifting his arms straight out from his side.

"Come on, wind… spirit," he whispered quietly enough that Sean wouldn't hear him. "Let's give him something memorable."

Instead of slithering through the grass like it did last time, the wind pounced on Xander like a lion. It roared into the field and crashed into Xander. He staggered as the wind took up a dance around him.

He quickly opened his eyes as a wall of wind formed around him, swirling like the birth of a tornado. The grass around him stood strangely still but the wind filled the rest of the field. Every exhaled breath came out of Xander's mouth in a puff of smoke as the temperature plummeted around him.

As the wind swirled faster and faster, he saw cans

and bottles emerging from the grass. Like puppets being controlled by a skillful marionette, the debris danced in the wind. It got caught up in the swirling madness and became part of the ever-expanding swirl of air.

Xander's ears popped as the air pressure increased. He tried to call out for Sean, or even laugh at the excitement of the moment, but the maddening wind stole away his words as soon as they left his mouth. Instead, he tilted his head back and laughed silently into the swirling maelstrom.

The increased air pressure drew the heavier objects out of the tall weeds. A rusted hubcap emerged, followed by a dilapidated car radiator. They joined the rest of the debris in its swirl, spinning in increasingly fast circles as the whipping wind reached near gale-force strength.

The hubcap flew dangerously close to him as it spun past. It was gone from his peripheral vision as quickly as it had appeared. When it reappeared, it was quite a bit further away, nearly to the distant trees. Like a projectile shot out of a cannon, the hubcap slammed into one of the trees, embedding itself deeply into the coarse wood.

Startled, Xander broke his concentration. For a moment, the cans and bottles slowed their spin before hanging in the air. They collapsed onto the ground as the last of the magic dissipated from the air.

"Sean?" Xander called out, suddenly worried for his friend. If the hubcap had enough force to bury itself into the thick wood, he was worried about what any of the other smaller items would have done to his friend.

"Sean!"

"That was so freaking cool," Sean yelled, emerging from behind one of the trees. "That was so freaking cool!"

Xander sighed happily at the sight of his heavyset friend. "See, I told you hiding behind the tree was a good idea."

"That was so freaking cool!" Sean yelled again as he bounded through the thick grasses. He crashed into Xander, enveloping him in a bear hug. "How did you do that?"

"I don't know." He saw his friend's disbelieving look and he raised his hands defensively. "I honestly don't know. I'd never done anything like this before yesterday."

"Oh my God," Sean said, covering his mouth in surprise. "The guy and the bus. That was you. You saved that guy's life."

"Maybe," he said. "Maybe I did. I don't really know."

"You've got to show me how you do it."

"I don't know how I do it. I don't think I could teach you even if I wanted to."

"It was so cool," Sean blurted. "What was it you did with the bus? F-5 strength winds that blew him out of the way? Increased air pressure that made the bus slow down sooner?"

"I don't know. I think I was thinking about a car's air bag. I think I made, like, a bubble of air between him and the bus."

"A bubble," Sean repeated dejectedly. "You have super powers and you're busy making a bubble? Couldn't you just fly in and save him or call down lightning on the bus or something?"

"You read too many comic books," Xander said as he started walking through the field.

Sean didn't follow and stared at his retreating friend. "Don't take this away from me. I'm best friends with a real-life superhero. The least you can do is let me live vicariously through you."

Xander stopped walking and sighed. "I'm not a superhero. Come on and catch up."

Sean jogged alongside him again.

Xander smiled despite himself. "It was pretty cool though, wasn't it? It was an air bubble. I made an air bubble between the guy and the bus. He bounced off it like a balloon."

"Okay. I'll admit that your super bubble power isn't entirely lame."

Xander brushed his dark hair out of his eyes and frowned. "Don't you think it's weird, though? I don't even know where these powers came from or why they suddenly appeared yesterday."

"Who cares? You're the only guy I know that would complain about becoming a superhero."

"I'm not a superhero."

"Whatever you say. So what do you think? Cape or no cape? And what color tights were you thinking about for your costume? I was thinking the Superman underwear on the outside of your outfit."

Xander punched him in the arm.

"You could always ask your parents if they know where you got your powers," Sean offered, rubbing the spot where he was punched. "Most of the time in the comic books, it's inherited."

"Yeah, that'll go over well. 'So Dad, I noticed I got your eyes. And Mom, I got your hair. Which one of you gave me the ability to control the wind?' I think I'll pass on that conversation. Anyway, I think they're planning on kicking me out of their house."

"Harsh. What did you do?"

"Me? Why is it something that I did?"

"Because you're a junior in college and you still live with your parents. You're pretty much a screw up by default."

"And my grandpa."

Sean smiled. "Yeah, you live with your parents and your grandpa. You know if you ever get kicked out, you're more than welcome to come crash at my apartment."

Xander smiled. "I may just have to take you up on that sooner than you think."

"Forget about that for now." Sean stopped walking and looked at his friend mischievously. "Want to see what else you can do with that power of yours?"

"Hell yeah, I do."

By the time Xander returned home later that night, he was exhausted and just wanted to go to bed. He opened the front door quietly but could hear the ensuing argument from the kitchen as soon as he entered the house.

"Quit being a coward, Jack!" his grandfather yelled in a much louder voice than Xander would have believed. "What are you going to do? Keep him hidden away in the house until he dies of old age?"

"If that's what it takes," his dad retorted. "What's the alternative? I let him grow up like we did? Moving every couple years because you pissed off someone new?"

"It's his right to choose."

"His right to choose? He can't even decide on a major after two and a half years of college. How do you expect him to make life-altering decisions like this?"

Xander crept through the foyer until he was near the doorway leading into the kitchen. He could see the two men standing at the far end of the breakfast nook, their arms flailing as they spoke and fingers being pointed angrily at one another.

"You may not have the chance to tell him the truth for much longer," his grandfather accused. "If I know about him, you can guarantee *they* do too."

"They're still trapped," his dad said quietly. The fire seemed to have left his side of the argument.

"Not all of them and you know it. They're only trapped as long as we exist but there are fewer of us than ever before. They're slipping out of their prison. It's only a matter of time before they come for us all, Xander included."

Xander's heart raced as he spied on the two men. From his vantage point, he could see his father's expression. Jack Sirocco always prided himself on being a stalwart breadwinner for his family. Few things, if anything, unnerved his father. From what he could see, however, his father was genuinely scared.

Anger welled inside Xander. Whatever they were discussing, he should be involved. If there was danger— and he wasn't foolish enough to believe that the danger and his newfound power were mutually exclusive—then he should be allowed to make the decisions about his life.

Xander stepped into the kitchen, making sure his shoes struck the tiled floor loudly enough to get everyone's attention. Both men turned toward Xander and immediately turned a deep scarlet from surprise and embarrassment.

"Would someone like to tell me what exactly is going on?" he demanded.

The two men looked at one another but neither spoke.

"Let me help you start," Xander growled in frustration. "You're sitting in this house making decisions about my future without having the common decency of explaining to me what exactly is going on. What were you guys talking about? Who are '*they*'?"

Xander's father stepped forward and rubbed his hands together nervously. "It's not that simple, son."

"Yes, it is," he replied, taking a step back as his father approached. He didn't want fatherly affection. He wanted answers.

"You're not old enough for this," his grandfather added cryptically. "You shouldn't even be going through this yet."

Xander turned in disbelief. "You too, Grandpa? I figured if anyone would have been on my side, it would have been you. Wasn't it you just this morning who wanted to talk about something important?"

His father turned sharply on his grandfather, who merely shrugged unapologetically. For a moment, Xander looked back and forth between the two men before realizing that neither of them was going to speak.

"You can't even bring yourself to tell me the truth, can you? Fine, then let me save you the trouble from having to worry about this later. I'm sick of this—you guys talking around me like I'm a child. I'm moving out. Then you can have as many mysterious conversations about my future as you want."

He looked sternly at his grandfather. "How's that for being old enough?"

"That's not what I meant," his grandfather began, but Xander was already walking out of the kitchen.

"Stop him," he heard his grandfather whisper harshly.

"Maybe this is for the best," his father replied dejectedly.

Xander stormed upstairs and slammed the door to his room. He leaned back heavily against it and bit back the wave of emotion that rolled over him. The tears that threatened to fall were more from sheer frustration than from sadness. At twenty years of age, he had hoped that he would no longer be treated like a child but it was clear that his family would never see him as a man.

He stuffed some clothes into a bag. He looked around his room and considered taking more, either his art supplies or some of the other items from his room. Eventually, he decided against it. The room, frozen as it was from his high school years, was as much a reminder of the way his family viewed him. If he were making a break, it would be from everything.

When he walked downstairs, his grandfather was standing by the door.

"Don't do this, Xander. It's dangerous out there, especially right now."

"You mean it's dangerous for a child like me," Xander retorted angrily. "That's what you said in the kitchen, right?"

"I'm obviously not going to be able to talk you out of leaving but take a piece of advice, won't you?"

Xander stood stoically but didn't interrupt.

"Don't trust anyone, Xander." His grandfather leaned close and Xander could smell the sweat on the old man's skin. "The only person you can trust right now is yourself. If it feels wrong, if it feels dangerous, run. Just run. You get into trouble—you come here and find me. Understand?"

"No, I don't," Xander said quietly.

His grandfather leaned back and placed his hand on the door. "You will."

He opened the door, allowing Xander to leave the house.

CHAPTER 4

"**D**o it again," Sean demanded as he set the empty two-liter soda bottles back up on the half wall separating his living room from the kitchen.

Xander sat forward on the couch and breathed deeply, letting the sensation of weightlessness wash over him. The sensation always reminded him of what it must be like to fly freely through the air.

The air in the room swirled, fluttering the pair of napkins sitting on the coffee table. The breeze moved toward Xander, pulled like it was caught in an unseen gravitational pull. Between his open palms, it coalesced into a shimmering ball of pressurized air.

Looking up, Xander focused on the nearest empty bottle. With a flick of his wrist, the air bubble shot through the air and struck the bottle just below its narrow neck. The bottle tumbled off the half wall and clattered onto the kitchen floor.

Xander turned his hand skyward and the bubble froze a few feet beyond the wall. Curling his fingers, the ball shot back and struck both the remaining bottles.

With a sigh, Xander released the pressurized wind. Both his and Sean's ears popped with the sudden change of pressure in the room.

"I stand corrected," Sean said, still chuckling excitedly. "Bubbles are way cooler than I ever would have believed."

He left the bottles on the floor and took a seat beside Xander on the couch. "You're really starting to get the hang of your super power."

Xander smiled wearily. "Will you stop calling them super powers?"

"Whatever. All I'm saying is that I'm rooming with a guy who can control the wind. That's pretty cool."

Xander scowled at his small bag of clothes dropped haphazardly beside the couch which, for the past couple days, had doubled as his bed. He was greatly appreciative of Sean letting him stay with him but he was still bitter toward his family for what he saw as a betrayal of his trust.

"Sorry," Sean said, noting Xander's expression. "Still too soon?"

"No, forget about it. Thanks for letting me crash here, though."

"No problem. What are best friends for?"

Sean leaned back and pulled apart some of the blinds. Night had settled hours ago. It was a moonless night, leaving the neighborhood cast in gloomy darkness. Only a pair of street lamps cast a glow on the broad parking lot outside the apartment building.

Dropping the blind, he looked down at his watch. "You know, it's still pretty early. You want to practice some more before we turn in for the night?"

Xander smiled, his sour disposition quickly

forgotten. "Yeah, I do."

Sean got back off the couch and walked over to the pair of fallen bottles on their side of the half wall.

"We have class tomorrow," Sean remarked as he set the first bottle onto the wall.

"Uh huh," Xander replied. He flexed his fingers in anticipation.

"You think Sammy's going to be there?"

Xander looked away but couldn't conceal his smile. Despite the distraction his newfound powers offered, he couldn't stop thinking about Sammy. Every curve of her face, every sparkle in her blue eyes, and every playful toss of her long hair was seared into his memory.

"I'll take that as a yes," Sean said as he set the second bottle onto the wall. "So, what are you going to do about Jessica?"

Xander's coy smile quickly evaporated. "What do you mean?"

"Come on. It's not exactly a big secret that you're infatuated with the new girl. You may say that Jessica is just your 'pseudo-girlfriend', but I'm pretty sure she thinks it's a little more important than that. You really think she's the type that's going to be okay with you jumping on the newest thing to roll into town?"

Xander opened his mouth but quickly shut it again. He didn't know which part of Sean's comments offended him more but he had trouble refuting the simple truth. Jessica wasn't the type of girl to take that sort of rejection. He was suddenly far less excited about going to school the next day.

"Don't worry, buddy," Sean said as he retrieved the

last bottle. "I'll put my moves on Jessica and you'll just be a distant memory by the end of the day tomorrow."

Xander laughed and released the bubble he'd been creating while they spoke. It crashed into the first bottle and narrowly missed Sean's nose as his friend set the last one on the ledge.

Long after Sean had gone to bed that night, Xander sat on the couch with his textbooks spread before him on the coffee table. He picked up a packet of paper, looked at the list of assignments he should have had completed by Monday, and frowned as he read through the expansive list. Despite the piles of homework he had already completed in the past couple hours, a daunting amount of work still remained to be done.

Between exploring his new powers, his fight with his family, and Sammy, he hadn't spent a lot of time concentrating on his schoolwork. Xander sighed as he dropped the syllabus back onto the stack of other paperwork. In that respect, his father had been right. Xander wasn't thinking about what really mattered and it was ruining his future.

He flipped open the nearest textbook and read through the first of many chapters he needed to read. The coffee cup steamed with the newest batch of freshly brewed coffee—one of many pots he expected to drink before the night was through. He might become a walking zombie by the time the next morning rolled around but he was determined to at least turn in the appropriate stack of homework when he got to class.

The chapter was predictably dry reading and he found himself re-reading the same paragraph two to three times before he fully absorbed the material. Glancing up at the clock, Xander saw the glaring green of the digital numbers reading just after midnight. Sighing, he turned the first textbook back to the first chapter and pulled out his homework questions.

"What is the longest railroad in the world, connecting Moscow to Pyongyang?"

He flipped forward a few pages to confirm his answer. As he ran his finger down the page, his eyes fell on the Trans-Siberian Railway. Grabbing his pencil, he copied down the answer. For a moment, Xander's eyes fell back to the textbook before he looked back to his homework and prepared to answer the second question. He immediately noticed something wrong with the answer he had copied down.

Xander picked up the paper so that he could see it more clearly through his weary eyes. Despite his mind screaming that the answer should have read "Trans-Siberian", his eyes told him the truth.

"Trans-Sammy Railway?" Xander read, dumbfounded.

He flipped his pencil around angrily—glad he chose to answer the questions in pencil rather than pen. He erased the answer and wrote down the correct one.

Xander's eyes fell on one of the homework assignments he had already completed and he let out a loud groan. The top answer started with "Sammy-economic evolution during the early 20th century…"

Panicked, he pulled up another random sampling

of his homework. Her name appeared in nearly every answer he had completed.

"General Sammy Jackson led the Confederate…"

"…which was later renamed Thailand from the previous Sammy…"

"…the article was clearly written with a Conservative Sammy…"

Xander dropped the stack of papers back onto the coffee table and rubbed his cheeks. The sensation against his growing beard was the only thing that confirmed he wasn't experiencing some horrible nightmare.

"I just met her two days ago," he moaned. "Now I can't stop thinking about her. What is going on?"

Xander dreaded every step he climbed toward the lecture hall. He wasn't necessarily passive-aggressive but he didn't like confrontation if it was avoidable. Unfortunately, he knew he couldn't avoid it when it came to Jessica. It was one of her personality flaws that had always kept her in the "pseudo-girlfriend" category, rather than him committing fully to their relationship.

He opened the back door to the room and saw Jessica's sorority sisters seated close together near the front of the room but he didn't see Jessica. Turning at the back row, his heart dropped quickly in his chest. There sat Jessica directly beside Sammy. Though they looked deep in conversation, Xander could easily read Sammy's pained expression.

"Hi ladies," he said disarmingly. He managed to keep a calmer exterior despite his jittery nerves.

"Hi sweetheart," Jessica said. Xander immediately felt like he was walking into a trap. "Pull up a seat and join us. I was just getting to know the new girl."

With Jessica's attention firmly on Xander and her back to Sammy, Sammy held up a piece of paper with the words SAVE ME printed in big letters across the page. Xander stifled a smile at the pleading sight.

His mirth disappeared when he looked at Jessica. He didn't see the flirtatious girl he'd known since freshman year. All he saw in her eyes was the overbearing sorority girl who was used to getting her way. The sight of that blatant arrogance made Xander irritated.

"What are you doing, Jessica?"

"I'm not doing anything. The new girl and I were just discussing what you and she talked about all during class on Friday."

Xander felt the hairs rise on the back of his neck. "First of all, her name is Sammy. You can at least fake civility and actually call her by her name. And second of all, it's none of your business what we talked about."

"I'm sorry," Jessica said as she stood from her chair. "I didn't mean to offend your girlfriend."

"She's not my girlfriend. She's a friend who happens to be a girl. But you know what? Right now, you are sure not acting like my friend and I'm not entirely sure I want you as a girlfriend."

Jessica's eyes narrowed dangerously. "Are you breaking up with me?"

"I can't break up with you, Jessica. We've never officially went out. You sit in the back of the room with me and flirt all day and then ask for my notes because you can't be bothered to take any. As for the other part, about you being a friend who's a girl, yeah, I guess I'm ending that too."

"What's gotten into you?" Jessica asked, genuine hurt reflected in her surprised expression. "This isn't you."

"Maybe it's just time someone told you the truth."

Xander mentally recoiled as Jessica flinched from his verbal barrage. While he couldn't condone the way she was talking to Sammy, she was right about his attitude. He normally avoided confrontation like this but the sight of Sammy being harassed by Jessica made him want to be the knight in shining armor that rode to Sammy's defense.

"Fine," Jessica sneered, her eyes glistening with tears. "Then maybe you can take her to the spring formal instead!"

Jessica shoved her way past him. Instead of turning toward her sorority sisters in the front of the room—all of whom were turned around and watching the scene unfold—she slammed open the back door and left the lecture hall.

Xander sighed in frustration and collapsed into the seat Jessica vacated, directly beside Sammy.

"She seems nice," Sammy said softly.

Despite his mood, Xander found himself smiling. "Yeah, she's swell."

They sat in silence while the room fell back into its normal rhythm. Slowly, all the other students turned around and returned to normal conversations before the professor arrived.

"Thanks," Sammy said finally.

"For what?"

"For standing up for me. Don't get me wrong—I can handle myself just fine. It's just… it's just nice to have someone stand up for you. You really are a nice guy."

"It's all a façade," Xander joked, his humor hiding the concern he felt for the way he talked to Jessica. She may be self-centered but she didn't deserve his condescension. "I'm just a normal college guy who's trying to get into your pants."

Sammy elbowed him playfully.

"I'm sorry," Xander said. "You didn't deserve to be pulled into the middle of our problems."

"Is there still an 'our' with you two?"

Xander looked over his shoulder to the closed door. "No, I guess there really isn't. I'm not entirely sure there ever was."

"You shouldn't have broken up with her for me."

"What makes you think that was all for you?"

Sammy arched a perfectly sculpted eyebrow. "Of course it was. All I'm saying is that you just met me. You don't even know me yet, not really."

"Are you an axe murderer?"

Sammy stared intently into his eyes. He could see the mischievous sparkle glistening. "I don't use an axe."

"Then so far so good. I guess the only solution left is to get to know you better." He had to steel himself before asking the question he'd wanted to ask since meeting her last week. "Maybe you'd like to go to dinner sometime?"

"I was thinking of something a little different. I was thinking that Jessica was right and you should ask me to the spring formal," she offered.

She quickly looked away, slightly embarrassed. Xander found the mix of brash confidence and coy modesty even more intoxicating.

"I'd love to take you to the formal."

Her smiled broadened in relief. "Then it's a date."

Xander returned her smile as his mind began to race. He didn't pay attention to a single thing the professor said during the lecture that day.

CHAPTER 5

*T*he White Halls Convention Center sounded far more remarkable than it truly was. The building, much like the rest of the town in which it resided, was anticlimactic when seen up close. Standing outside the glassed entryway, Xander thought it looked far more like a high school gymnasium. In a town like White Halls, however, there weren't a lot of better options when hosting an event as large as the spring formal.

The event was themed—Alice in Wonderland, as Xander noted from the myriad of posters and banners hung around the building—but he wasn't dressed for a part. He had rented a dark grey suit and tie, though the tie had been intentionally left behind in his car.

Other students filtered past him while he waited for Sammy. They wore assortments of bunny ears and stovepipe hats with hand-drawn playing cards stuffed into ribbon bands around their brims. A few girls arrived in the traditional blue dress with white apron, though the sheer number of homegrown Alices made the outfit far from special. There was one remarkable Queen of Hearts that entered but she was really only remarkable because the outfit left little to the imagination. Some strategically placed hearts on the Queen of Hearts were the only solid pieces of fabric on the whole ensemble.

Xander waved to a few friends he recognized as they entered. Some of the men had dressed up as well but most were variations of the Mad Hatter.

He admired the costumes as an excuse to keep his mind busy and stop waiting impatiently for Sammy to arrive. Since their class together on Monday, he had thought of little else but her. Sean had even remarked at his lack of focus when experimenting with his new powers.

Xander reached up and scratched his stubbly chin. Not two weeks before, he had discovered the ability to control the wind. Yet even that seemed to pale in light of his infatuation for Sammy. Xander wasn't a stupid man. He could see that something was wrong. He had never been the type to grow infatuated with anyone. Even his attraction to Jessica had always been tempered with logic and common sense. Common sense had been the first thing to go when he met Sammy.

His attraction to her, he hated to admit, bordered on something supernatural.

Before he could follow that train of thought any further, his eyes saw a flicker of luscious blonde hair. Sammy wore a dress of layered lace that fell just above her knees. The upper part of her dress hugged her body like a corset before billowing again at the sleeves. Her milky skin flowed from the dress as she moved. Xander couldn't take his eyes off her.

As soon as she saw him, a smile broke across her face. She hurried up to him, slipping past the other couples that slowly moved inside the convention center.

Stopping just short, she placed her hands behind her back and smiled sheepishly up at him.

"Do you like my dress?"

Xander's mouth moved but he couldn't find the words. "You look amazing," he finally stammered.

Sammy blushed. "I wanted to go with a more contemporary Alice, something a little different from the blue and white."

"Mission accomplished," he said. "You look ready to dive down a rabbit hole."

"Maybe we can just start with a drink and dancing."

Xander offered his arm, which she quickly took, and led her inside. The inside of the convention center had been transformed into its own Wonderland. A snack table to the left as they entered offered tea and small pieces of cake. Despite the general corniness of the event, Xander was genuinely impressed with their details.

His attention, however, kept drifting back to Sammy. "You look amazing."

She smiled. "You said that already."

"It's worth repeating."

They found a couple open seats at one of the round tables. An assortment of drinks in various stages of consumption was spread around the table but their owners were busy on the dance floor. A cascade of conversation topics ran through Xander's head but he dismissed each in turn every time he looked at Sammy.

She looked over and caught him staring, not for the first time that night. "You're unusually quiet."

Xander cleared his throat and chose to take a sip

of his drink.

Sammy smiled. "Don't tell me you're the type of guy that only talks a good game right up to the point where the girl actually likes him."

"This is our first date," Xander finally said. "I don't want to scare you away just yet."

She placed her hand on his. Her skin seemed to burn against his clammy hand. "You're not going to scare me away. I'm a big girl. If you have something you want to say, just say it."

Xander turned his palm over and slid his fingers between hers. "This is going to be a horrible conversation piece for our first date but I really have to say it. Ever since I met you, I can't stop thinking about you. I don't want you to think I'm some crazy stalker or anything. This isn't even really me. I'm normally so standoffish and—"

Before he could continue, Sammy grabbed a hold of his lapel and pulled him into a kiss. Her lips were warm and smooth against his. She pulled back as quickly as she had begun.

"You talk too much," she said.

Xander's eyes were still closed but a smile was plastered across his face. "Yeah, you're probably right."

He risked opening an eye and caught sight of her coy smile. He suddenly felt more relaxed than he had in weeks.

"Do you want to dance?" he said.

She stood without saying a word and, with their hands still interlocked, pulled him onto the dance floor.

He felt awkward pushing their way past the dancing students. He wasn't the best dancer and the fast pace of the music currently playing left him very self-aware.

The song that was playing ended as they reached the center of the dance floor. The flashing multi-colored lights shut off and the room was cast into a dim glow. From the speakers around the room, a gentle melody began.

Sammy slipped her arms around his neck and laid her head on his shoulder. He slipped his hands around the small of her back and she let herself sink into him as they danced.

Xander wasn't sure how long the song actually lasted. It couldn't have been more than three or four minutes, but it felt like a blissful eternity while they shared their moment on the dance floor.

When the song finally ended, they both seemed satisfied and walked back to the table. Someone had walked around the room during the slow dance and lit candles in each of the centerpieces. The Wonderland decorations became hauntingly beautiful in the dim candlelight. Patterns danced on the faux trees. The cardboard smoke rings from the caterpillar's pipe seemed to sway in an unseen breeze.

Before Xander could admire the ambiance for too long, Sammy nudged him to get his attention. Following her gaze, Xander frowned deeply. Jessica was walking purposefully through the crowd, followed closely by a stocky football player whom Xander only mildly recognized.

Jessica's expression told him that her civility would be kept to a bare minimum. After the amazing evening he'd had thus far, the last thing he wanted was a confrontation with her.

"Let's just leave," Xander offered.

"No," Sammy said adamantly. "There are some things that probably need to be said before we go."

Jessica and her date stopped at the far edge of the table. The rounded table offered just enough distance between the two couples that physical contact was an impossibility, though Jessica's spite knew no such bounds.

"That's an awfully cute dress," she said wickedly. "Did you make it yourself?"

Sammy stared at her but didn't reply. Xander felt like the temperature in the room had suddenly been turned up by a few dozen degrees. Sweat began beading on his forehead and he was glad he had an undershirt to catch the moisture beginning to roll down his back.

"You know what?" Jessica continued. "You don't have to answer that. I'd rather you didn't talk right now and let me say what I have to say. I don't know who you are. I don't even know your last name."

Xander frowned slightly. He was on a date with Sammy and he just realized that he didn't know her last name either.

"But since you've shown up," Jessica said, leaning across the table as far as the space would allow, "you've caused me nothing but trouble. I happen to be president of the largest sorority on campus. If I wanted to, I could make your life a living hell. And you may think to yourself that no one is that petty—but you'd be *wrong*."

She leaned back a little, having said what she needed to say. "Now, is there anything you'd like to say before I walk away from here? An apology, maybe?"

Sammy nodded softly. "Your dress is on fire."

Jessica looked down in horror as a small flame ignited the end of her sleeve. She screamed and her date grabbed the nearest drink and threw it on her. The cranberry juice soaked the entire front of her dress, staining the white apron. Jessica's wrath toward Sammy was immediately forgotten as she stormed furiously away, her date trailing further and further behind.

"That was the best rebuttal I've ever heard," Xander said in awe. "I don't even think she realized she'd leaned across the candle."

"I certainly wasn't going to tell her," Sammy joked, though the humor felt strained.

"Are you okay? That was a little harsh, even from Jessica."

Sammy nodded. "Do you mind if we just get out of here? I don't really think I want to be around when she gets back."

"You got somewhere in mind?" he asked.

"I don't live that far away," she said. "Maybe you can walk me home."

The cool night air felt wonderful against Xander's flushed face. They hadn't spoken since leaving the convention center but he was satisfied without meaningless conversation. They walked hand in hand, strolling down the vacant and quiet streets of White Halls.

He didn't recognize the part of town through

which they walked but that wasn't entirely unusual. The town was pretty well separated by College Street and he rarely had a reason to come to this side of the small town.

Looking over, he saw Sammy's distant stare. The jovial attitude he'd come to appreciate over the past week seemed curiously absent, as though she had a lot weighing on her mind.

"Penny for your thoughts?" he asked.

She shook her hair and reached up with her far hand. She brushed some of her hair out of her face but he swore she also wiped the corner of her eyes as though wiping away a tear.

Xander stopped and pulled at her hand, forcing her to stop as well. "What's wrong? You're not still bothered by Jessica, are you? I told you that you shouldn't worry about her."

"It's not Jessica," she replied sadly. "You're just such a nice guy and you treat me so well. You're just so different from what I expected when we met."

"Shouldn't that make you happy?"

"It should," she conceded. "I'm just not a good person, Xander, I'm really not. I'm going to break your heart and you're going to hate me."

"Unless you tell me that our first date was really horrible or I'm a terrible kisser, I don't think you're going to break my heart."

His attempt at humor elicited little more than a weak smile. Sammy looked down at her feet, unable to even make eye contact.

"Our date wasn't all that bad, was it?"

"No, it was perfect." She seemed nearly on the

verge of tears.

"Then what is it?"

Sammy pointed to an abandoned house across the street. The windows were boarded over but someone had removed the planks from the front door. With only a few interspersed street lamps on the road, the house looked dark and foreboding.

"Come with me," she said softly. "I have to show you something."

He followed without question, eager to find out what was bothering her so badly. "You don't live here, do you?"

She squeezed his hand as she led him across the street.

The front door opened with an ear-piercing screech as the rusted hinge fought against the intrusion. The smell of dust and mold assaulted his senses and he had to bite back a sneeze. A few footprints crisscrossed across the foyer but they looked old. New layers of dust and dirt had already settled into those ancient steps.

The hardwood floors groaned with each step they took, betraying the otherwise stagnant air of the abandoned house. Looking around, Xander appreciated what the house once represented. Despite most of the crystal having been stripped away, he could still tell that the chandelier above the staircase was impressive.

"Why are we here?"

Sammy didn't reply but led him to the staircase heading upstairs. He could see her shoulders heave with emotion as she walked and a sense of dread settled into his gut. Good news didn't come from an emotional woman in a decrepit building.

Each stair creaked in turn as they climbed the stairs. Debris—a collection of empty cans and stained bottles—littered the first stairwell landing. On the upper floor, he could see small scorch marks against the wall where the wallpaper had bubbled and peeled against the heat. More empty cans sat nearby, remnants of what Xander had to assume were small cooking fires.

Sammy led him to a back room, the door of which was already ajar. As they stepped inside, she turned toward him. Her eyes sparkled with tears and the mascara had run at the corners of her almond eyes. The sight was heartbreaking and he only wanted to reach out and comfort her.

"Wait here," she said, placing a hand gently on his chest.

The room was empty, aside from the pair of young lovers. A set of windows was cut into the far wall but plywood had been placed over the glass ages ago. Only faint slivers of light from the streetlamps outside filtered around the edges of the wood and softly illuminated the room.

Sammy walked to the center of the room before stopping, her back facing him. Her shoulders rose and fell as she took deep breaths. Xander looked around, wondering what all this was about. He was so consumed with his curiosity that he almost missed her gentle whisper.

"I'm sorry, Xander," she said in a barely audible voice. "I'm really sorry."

She spun on her heel and the room suddenly

illuminated with vibrant reds, oranges, and yellows. With a flick of her wrist, a ball of flame leapt from her hand and flew across the room.

Her aim was slightly off and the ball struck the wall just beside Xander, showering him and the room in a blossom of sparks. He could smell the pungent aroma of sulfur mixed with the toxic scent of melting wallpaper and plaster.

Her hands were sheathed in flames and the flickering colors were reflected in her smoldering eyes.

Reflexively, Xander raised his hand and the room was filled with swirling wind. The flames on her arms danced wildly in the wind, alternating growing smaller against the breeze before flaring even brighter as it burned away the oxygen in the room.

Sammy raised an arm defensively in front of her face. The power swelled inside Xander, seeming to feed off his fear and adrenaline. As the wind flowed through him, he felt it pressurizing around her. He closed his hands into a sphere in front of him as he squinted against the gale-force winds.

As quickly as they had begun, the winds died. The glow from the fires diminished as well as Xander realized that Sammy was completely encased in an air bubble.

She stared at him through the shimmering bubble but it wasn't with animosity like he had expected. Her expression was deeply colored with sadness.

"What is going on?" Xander yelled as he approached the bubble.

"I'm sorry, Xander," she cried. Tears rolled down her cheek. "I don't have a choice."

Pockets of flame began to ignite around her arms again but she had to cough as smoke began filling the bubble.

"I wouldn't do that," he said, feeling horribly deflated. "If you don't burn all the oxygen out of the bubble, I'll pull all the air out and let you suffocate."

She looked at him again and bit back a body-wracking sob. The flames on her arms were reabsorbed into her skin, leaving them both in relative darkness.

He wanted to rail against her but all he could hear were her continued sobs. His mind fell time and time again to the flames that had engulfed her, seemingly without harm.

"Why?" he asked quietly.

She reached up and wiped away her tears with the back of her hand. "I don't have a choice. I'm a Fire Warrior. I had to do this."

"I don't understand. What is a Fire Warrior? Why did you have to attack me?" He felt his ire growing. "You could have killed me!"

"I couldn't," she blurted out in the darkness. "I was supposed to. I was supposed to bring you here and kill you but I couldn't. Please, you have to believe me. I couldn't do it!"

Xander felt crestfallen, like he had been stabbed in the chest. This woman who he had fallen for so completely was his assassin.

"So this was all a lie. You toyed with me just to get me here?"

"Yes. No," she cried out in the darkness and it took her a long moment to regain her composure. "I was supposed to get close enough to you to get you here. That was it. But we have a real connection. I know you feel it too and it's way more than just love at first sight."

"Stop," he demanded.

"There's something tangible and unnatural between us. I know you can feel it!"

"Just stop!"

He wanted her to stop talking, not because he was angry with her but because he knew she was right. Whatever they felt for one another transcended simple puppy love or physical attraction.

His eyes finally adjusted to the gloom of the abandoned house and he could see her puffy eyes and streaks of tears that had been traced down her face. The woman he was staring at might be a liar but she wasn't a killer.

With a wave of his hand, he dismissed the air bubble.

Sammy stared at him in surprise but he spoke before she could say anything else that would hurt him.

"Just explain to me why? Why did you have to do this?"

She stared at him as though he had asked her a trick question. When she realized he was serious, she tried to stammer through an answer.

"It's the cycle of the elements. Earth gives way to the sea, the sea bows to the wind, the wind feeds the flame, and the flame burns the world of man down to the earth."

Xander stared at her sternly. "You're not making any sense."

"The time of the Wind Caste is coming to an end. It's the time for the Fire Caste to take over."

"You're not making any sense!"

"You're a Wind Warrior!" she cried.

He shook his head. A part of his gut twisted as his mind began theorizing about the truth.

"What's a Wind Warrior? What's the Wind Caste?"

Sammy staggered in surprise. "You really don't know, do you? This wasn't all just an act. You really have no idea." Her hand flew to her mouth as she stifled another cry. "Oh my God, I almost killed you and you don't even know the truth."

"Please, Sammy. No more games. Tell me the truth."

"You're a Wind Warrior, Xander. You can control the wind like a weapon. Your kind has protected the Earth for thousands of years but your time is coming to an end. It's time for the Fire Caste to take over."

"How..." he began, before choking back the question. He cleared his throat before continuing. "How does someone become a Wind Warrior?"

Sammy looked devastated as she told him the truth. "It's passed down through your family. Someone in your family had to be of the Wind Caste."

All the cryptic conversations between his father and grandfather came pouring through his mind. He stripped away every conversation he could remember, trying to put it into the context of what he had just been told. He felt his anger returning but not directed at Sammy.

"Go," he said, motioning toward the door.

"What?"

"Go. Run, before I change my mind."

Sammy didn't need a second invitation. She skirted well clear of Xander as she rushed to the door. He heard her footsteps pull up short of the doorway.

"You weren't like they said you'd be," she said. "They said you'd be evil—an oppressor who would stop at nothing to keep us from claiming our right to reign. You're a good man, Xander."

Xander refused to reply and kept his back to her, though her words burned him deeper than her fire ever could have.

"I have to warn you before I go," she said, the strength returning to her voice. "I didn't come alone. If you have any other Wind Warriors in your family, their lives are in danger. You need to go warn them."

Xander nodded without turning to face her.

She took another step but stopped and turned toward him again. "You wouldn't really have sucked all the air out of the bubble, would you?"

When he didn't reply, she turned sadly, walked down the stairs, and out of the house.

He waited until he was sure she was gone before he whispered into the room, "No, I wouldn't have."

His anger was reignited when he thought about his family and the lies they'd told him. He wasn't entirely sure he could make the same promise to them.

CHAPTER 6

The car idled in the driveway as Xander leaned back against the driver's seat. He lifted his head and stared at his parent's house. The lights in both the living room and dining room were on and he assumed they were sitting around the table after dinner. A sense of betrayal washed over him as he stared at the unassuming house. His parents had gotten him ready for school every day of his life, sat around the table during meals, and tucked him in at night. The entire time they knew what he was and hadn't told him.

It's passed down through your family, Sammy had told him. As much as she had betrayed his trust as well, he had no reason to doubt her.

He turned off the engine and climbed out of the car. The night air seemed far cooler than it had been during the spring formal. A wind gusted around his legs, pulling at his suit pants. Xander frowned, suddenly not sure if the wind was natural or if he was creating it as a response to his bad mood.

The porch steps creaked as he climbed to the front door. He knew it would be unlocked; his parents rarely locked it until they were going to bed.

He turned the handle and the door swung open.

Xander could hear the chairs being pushed back from the dining room table as the door opened, his family curious about their unannounced guest.

His father was the first one around the corner but his mother and grandfather followed closely behind.

"Xander, thank God," his father said. "We've been worried sick about you."

"Have you?" he replied harshly.

His father seemed taken aback. He stopped in the hallway and stared at his son. "Of course we were worried. We haven't heard from you since you left the other day. We wanted to make sure you were okay."

"I'm not okay, Dad. I'm angry and I'm hurt."

"What are you talking about?" his mother asked, stepping up beside her husband.

"What's a Wind Warrior?"

The silence in the house seemed deafening. No one spoke but their expressions confirmed what Xander suspected all along. Slowly, his father turned toward his grandfather and they shared a knowing expression.

"Where did you hear that?" his father asked, surprisingly calm for the situation.

"From a Fire Warrior who tried to kill me tonight!"

"A Fire Warrior," his grandfather said, though his inflection didn't turn it into a question as much as a statement of fact.

Xander turned his attention back to his father. "You knew what I was this whole time, didn't you?" He didn't wait for a response before he continued berating his father. "I could have been killed tonight all because you were too egocentric to bother to tell me the truth! You could have been training me to use my powers! You could have been helping me prepare before something like this happened!"

"No, he couldn't," his grandfather said sadly. "He couldn't because he's not the Wind Warrior. I am."

Xander felt deflated. "You?"

"It follows family lines but not every member of a family becomes one. It skipped your father. He's just a normal man, like you were until a couple weeks ago."

"Why?" Xander asked, unable to find a more articulate question. "Why didn't you tell me the truth?"

"Because I asked him not to," his father said. "I grew up the son of a Wind Warrior and it was a living hell for me. Your grandfather had a perpetual obligation to save the world but he never thought about what his responsibilities did to our family. We'd settle somewhere new and your grandfather would go off to right some wrong in the world. Next thing you knew, someone would claim they saw him flying through the air or making a hurricane to put out a forest fire. And just like that, we'd have to pack up our things and move somewhere new, somewhere where no one knew us so we could start a new life. I moved six times during high school alone. Six times!"

His father looked exhausted and aged. "I didn't want that for you, Xander. I wanted you to have a normal life. You don't know how hard it's been for me since I found out you were one of them."

"How hard it's been for you?" Xander replied. He empathized with his father's sadness but couldn't ignore the fact that everyone seemed far more interested in controlling his life then letting him choose for himself.

"What else did the Fire Warrior say before you killed him?" his grandfather asked.

"It was a she and I didn't kill her."

"You let her go? Even weakened like the Fire Caste is right now, she's still a danger."

"She's not a danger to us. But she did say there were others with her that are looking for the rest of the Wind Warriors."

"If there's more," his grandfather quickly said to his father, "then we need to get out of the house."

"This is exactly what I didn't want," his father replied angrily. "Even now, after all these years, your life is ruining everyone else's. Have you ever thought that maybe we don't want to pack up our lives and leave? We have a good life here!"

"Don't be a fool, Jack! You think the Fire Warriors care about the life you have?"

Xander shook his head sadly and turned back toward the front door. He slipped back outside before anyone even realized he was gone.

"Xander!" his grandfather yelled as the elder man hurried down the street to catch up.

Xander stuffed his hands deeper into his jacket pockets and kept walking. His grandfather caught up with a huff of exertion and fell into step beside his grandson.

"Come back to the house."

"I don't think so. You all have been lying to me my entire life. You, more than anyone."

"Then where will you go?"

"Anywhere but here."

"Quit being such a little kid, Xander. I know you're angry right now but your life is in danger."

Xander stopped walking and turned toward the old man. "Don't you think I know that? I took a girl out on a date and she tried to set me on fire. No one knows the danger I'm in better than me."

"I'm… I'm sorry. You shouldn't even be going through this yet."

Xander furrowed his brow. "That's the second time you've told me I'm too young."

"That's because you are. Wind Warriors are born with our powers but they don't manifest until you turn twenty-five. I don't know why you suddenly got your powers so early. It doesn't make sense. But if you got them, there's a reason."

Xander's thoughts drifted to Sammy. He knew some people looked deceptively young but he doubted she was twenty-five either.

"What reason could there be for ruining my life?"

"Quit being a drama queen, boy," his grandfather growled. "You may not appreciate it but you've been given a great honor."

"I don't appreciate it because I'm apparently the only person that doesn't know what the hell is going on."

"Sit," his grandfather said, pointing to a bench on the outskirts of a city park. "Sit and I'll try to explain it to you."

Xander hesitated as the older man took a seat on the bench. With a sigh, he walked over and joined his grandfather.

"So what is a Wind Warrior?"

"You've already figured it out. We can control the wind—shape it into whatever we want it to be."

"No, I understand that part. I mean what *is* a Wind Warrior? Why do we even exist?"

"To explain it in the simplest terms possible, we're the guides for humanity. We're part of one of the four elements: earth, water, air, and fire. Those four elements exist in the four elemental castes. You're a part of the Wind Caste."

"And Sammy is a part of the Fire Caste."

"Exactly. The Wind Caste served as the spiritual guides for humanity, inspiring them to reach for the heavens. We were the wise old men sitting on mountaintops dispensing advice."

"No," Xander joked, his humor serving as a defense mechanism when he grew increasingly nervous. "You're just an old man sitting on a park bench."

"I used to be so much more. I gave it up."

"Why?"

"Because your father was right. I was a terrible dad to him growing up, always putting the duties of the caste above my duties as a father. I think he knew that I was disappointed when he didn't become a Wind Warrior. I swore that it wasn't too late to be a decent father, so I became a father and grandfather rather than a warrior."

Xander was surprised by the depth of his

grandfather's answer. He never considered the sacrifices the elder man had made—first for the caste and then after for his family.

"So if we're Wind and Sammy is Fire, then there are whole other groups of Earth and Water Warriors running around too, right? How come I've never heard anything about them?"

His grandfather shook his head. "Because there are no Earth or Water Warriors left. There wasn't even a Fire Caste until a few decades ago."

Xander sat forward on the bench. "Where did the others go?"

"They died."

Xander looked mortified but his grandfather dismissed his concerns with a soft chuckle.

"No one killed them, if that's what you're thinking. Each element serves its purpose, helping the evolution of the planet, but no two castes ever exist at the same time."

Xander remembered something Sammy had said in the dilapidated house. "Earth gives way to the sea, the sea bows before the wind—"

"—the wind feeds the flame, and the flame burns the world of man back to the earth. I see you've heard it before."

"Sammy said it to me—the Fire Warrior."

"Well, she's a smart girl. Dangerous but smart."

"If no two castes can exist at the same time, how can there be Fire Warriors now?"

His grandfather looked solemn. "I think you can figure out that answer."

"It's because our time is coming to an end, isn't

it?" he sighed.

The old man nodded. "There used to be thousands of us but we've slowly been growing old and passing on without leaving new Wind Warriors to take our place. You're the first new Wind Warrior in over twenty years."

"How many of us are left?"

"Too few," his grandfather replied sadly. "Far too few. The Fire Caste has been born because our era is nearing its end."

"Wait, the prophecy says that the flames burn the world of man. What does that mean?"

The elder shrugged. "Exactly what it says. Don't look so surprised. Nearly every religion has a prophecy about the end times, when the Earth as we know it is destroyed and reborn anew. Christians have Revelations. The Norse had Ragnarok. This is just our version of the same story."

Xander stood and turned toward his grandfather. He couldn't believe the man he'd known all his life, the man who showed so much compassion for everyone he met, was so calm about the end of the world.

"They're planning on destroying the world. How are they not our mortal enemies?"

"Because they're not," his grandfather replied gruffly. "They're not evil people. They're fulfilling their role in the natural cycle of evolution."

Xander leaned forward until his face was inches from the old man's. "No, they're not. They're trying to kill us. There's nothing natural about that."

"I will admit that trying to kill us isn't part of the plan. It sounds to me like there's an offshoot of the Fire

Warriors who don't want to wait their turn, especially with a new Wind Warrior being activated after so many years. Before you, they might have just been content waiting out their turn for a few more decades."

"How do they even know about me?" he said, walking away from the bench and staring up at the clear night's sky.

"The same way I knew about you. We're all connected through the elements. When one of us uses our abilities, everyone else can sense it. We used to use that ability whenever a new Wind Warrior reached the age so that we could bring them into the fold. I guess it makes sense that Fire Warriors have the same connection to us, though that's just speculation."

Xander cursed himself quietly for being so stupid. Everything made a lot more sense now. Sammy had shown up to his class the day after he saved that man from being hit by the bus. She had to have sensed his power and was sent immediately afterward. How could he have been so blind?

He sighed and turned back to his grandfather. "So what do we do now?"

"We run. We get as far away as we can and we keep you safe."

"And then what? Never use our powers again? We know they can track us—so we just all live to a ripe old age until we die of natural causes and the Fire Caste takes over?"

"I didn't say it was a good plan."

"And what happens when they do take over? What happens to the Earth?"

His grandfather shrugged. "As each of the Wind Warriors die, I would assume volcanoes would erupt. There would be city-shattering earthquakes. When the last of us pass on, the Fire Warriors will be able to fully escape their prison and roam the Earth."

Xander shook his head. "Then I'm not running. I can't hide and save myself while knowingly damning the rest of the world."

"You're a stubborn mule of a boy, you know that?"

"I'm sure that's hereditary too," he replied with a smile. "So where do we find these Fire Warriors?"

His grandfather's smile washed from his face. Xander felt it too, a sudden surge of energy like the static charge just before a lightning strike.

From out of the trees in the park behind them, dark-robed men emerged. In their hands, burning orbs danced in the darkness.

"I don't think finding them will be a problem," the old man whispered.

CHAPTER 7

*H*is grandfather launched into the air, carried upward on a sudden gust of wind, just as the bench ignited in flames and sparks. The wind died when the old man was nearly twenty feet in the air, leaving him hovering as he redirected the wind flow. A sudden downdraft of pressurized air slammed into one of the Fire Warriors, driving the man into the ground with violent force.

"Run, Xander!" his grandfather yelled. "I'll hold them off."

"No way," Xander replied. "I can help."

He was stepping toward the dark-robed men when the ground in front of him erupted in a wall of flames. The flames burned nearly white with an intense heat that washed over him. Xander staggered backward as his clothes began to smolder and the air burned in his lungs.

He could barely see his grandfather land on the far side of the flames. He heard, rather than saw, a roar of a tornado as it touched down, uprooting one of the trees in the park. Xander saw the silhouette of a man being launched high into the night sky and didn't envy the painful landing he had in his future.

Beyond the wall of flame, sparks roared into the night air. Balls of flame exploded against the ground as they sought the agile old man. One of the Fire Warriors stretched out his hands and a jet of flame poured across the field. His grandfather rolled to the side but the flames ignited the side of his shirt. A quick arctic breeze froze the shirt and extinguished the flames but Xander could hear his grandfather's labored breathing over the din of battle.

He waved his hand and a futilely small gust of wind crashed against the wall of fire. Instead of breaking through, the wind only fed the flames that grew more intense in response.

Frustrated, Xander stepped further away. Maybe his grandfather was right? He barely knew how to control his powers. Maybe he was a bigger liability by sticking around. Maybe he should run, like his grandfather had asked.

A scream split the air, a throaty yell that sounded close to a mix of pain and coarse coughing. Xander knew that sound and the cough that accompanied it. His grandfather was hurt.

He closed his eyes and bit back the tears of frustration. "Please, I know you can hear me. You used me as a vessel when you helped save that man from the bus. Help me save another of your children. Use me however you have to, just save my grandfather!"

The wind turned from a faint breeze to a gusting hurricane that nearly knocked Xander from his feet. The wind blew from behind him but never passed his body. It poured into him like water into a pail, filling him quickly to the brim. The gusting wind whispered to him as it filled his essence, speaking in a language he didn't understand but telling a story he knew all too well. In that divine moment, Xander reached a point of celestial clarity.

With a wave of his hand, the wind crashed into the wall of flames. The fire swirled madly before burning down to hot coals on the ground. Xander stepped through, his eyes glowing a frigid white in the moonless night.

The Fire Warriors were frozen in a horseshoe around his grandfather, who knelt on one knee clutching his chest. Before the first Fire Warrior could turn toward the new threat, Xander formed a ball of air in his hand and whipped it outward. The ball crashed into the nearest warrior, lifting him from his feet and throwing him into the depths of the park. Xander heard him crash into a tree and heard the splintering of wood from the impact.

He easily turned the ball on the next Fire Warrior, striking him in the back and sending the warrior sprawling into the mud.

The rest of the Fire Warriors scattered as Xander continued his assault. From the corner of his eye, he saw a ball of flame soaring at him. A flick of his wrist turned the blowing wind into hurricane strength, which easily deflected the fireball. He turned the wind on the Fire Warrior that attacked him, sending him tumbling end over end into the woods.

"Stop right now!" a voice yelled from across the park.

Xander turned to the sound and found a warrior

holding his grandfather by the throat. In his other hand, fire roared between his fingertips. Xander could see the anguish on the old man's face and knew that even the hand that held him in place had to be hot enough to burn his flesh.

"Turn down the wind or I'll burn the old man to the ground."

The smoldering white in Xander's eyes faded and the wind that whipped his hair about receded into his body.

"What do you think you're doing here?" Xander asked, holding his arms out wide in a show of surrender.

"We're claiming what's ours," the Fire Warrior replied.

"By killing the Wind Caste? I may be new to this but I'm pretty sure that's not how it works."

The warrior laughed derisively. "And you think we should, wait another sixty years until you finally decided to have the decency to die? Lord Balor might have waited for this old man and his crew to pass on but you're something different. We won't wait for any longer before we take what's rightfully ours."

"It's not yours," Xander replied. "It's still mine! I just found out that there's this whole world that I never knew existed. I just found out I'm something far more special than just another slacker college student. I'm not about to give that up just yet."

"You can't stop us. Wind feeds the flame, remember? The best thing you could have done would have been to die when Sammy tried to kill you. Now you're going to die and she's going to suffer for her failure."

The mention of Sammy ignited a flame in Xander's chest. There was no reason why he should be so willing to protect her when she had clearly betrayed him, but the moment the warrior threatened her, he felt himself grow dangerously defensive.

"Not if I take away your fuel," Xander growled.

A bubble appeared around the Fire Warrior's hand. When Xander jerked both his hands backward, the air was sucked out of the bubble in jets of pressurized air. Without the oxygen to feed his flames, the fire on the warrior's hand disappeared in a puff of smoke.

"What did you—?"

The warrior couldn't finish his sentence as another bubble appeared around his head. Sammy had wondered if he could truly pull the oxygen from the bubble when he had her trapped. At the time, he wasn't sure it was even possible, much less if he could have done it to her as a punishment. In this instance, he felt significantly more confident and justified.

The air escaped the bubble in an audible gush. The Fire Warrior gasped for air that no longer existed in the personal vacuum around his head. His lungs screamed for relief as the oxygen was pulled from them as well. Three seconds later, as the lack of oxygen reached his brain, the Fire Warrior released Xander's grandfather and pitched forward, unconscious. Xander released the bubble before he hit the ground, making sure that the man lived while also making sure nothing blunted the impact as his face struck the ground.

"Who's next?" Xander yelled to the few remaining

warriors.

In response, they turned and ran into the woods, not eager to fight the newly minted Wind Warrior.

When he was sure it was safe, Xander rushed over to his grandfather's side. The old man propped himself up on a knee with his hand pressed against the ground. Xander slipped his grandfather's free arm over his shoulder and helped him to his feet.

"Can you walk?"

His grandfather nodded. "I've been through worse. Are any of them still around?"

Xander looked over his shoulder and shook his head. "There are some around but none that are in any condition to answer questions."

"They'll be back," the elder man groaned. "They'll come back with even more Fire Warriors and overwhelm us."

"What would you have me do?"

"We run, like we should have done in the beginning."

Xander shook his head. "You heard my dad. He won't leave White Halls."

"I know, Xander. I don't plan on taking him with us."

Xander would have stepped back in surprise if he hadn't been bearing so much of his grandfather's weight. "Just like that? You just want to leave them to face the Fire Caste alone?"

"The Fire Warriors don't care about your dad and mom. They're normals, not part of the Wind Caste. It's you and me that they want."

Xander looked over his shoulder and down the street. In the far distance, he could see the glowing porch light of the house he grew up in. Everything he'd ever known existed in that house and in this town. The thought of leaving White Halls scared him to death.

"Where will we go?" Xander asked.

"We'll join the others Wind Warriors. We'll need to warn them that the Fire Caste has declared war on our survivors anyway."

"The Fire Warrior mentioned a name—Lord Balor. Does that name mean anything to you?"

"No, but it wouldn't, would it? The Fire Caste didn't even exist when I was doing most of my work as a Wind Warrior. But we'll keep his name in mind. I don't think we've heard the last of him."

Xander's gaze fell once again on the house in the distance. Beyond their street, they could hear the police and fire sirens screaming into the quiet night. Around them, the few houses that existed on their rural street were coming to life, with lights turning on in the windows of curious onlookers.

"I know you want to say goodbye, Xander. Make it quick. We don't want to be here when the Fire Warriors come back and I sure don't know how to explain this to the police. We need to hurry."

His parents stood on the porch when Xander approached. He wasn't surprised to see the tears gleaming in his mother's eyes. His father's tears, however, startled him. His father didn't bother concealing his emotion and instead let the tears roll into his beard.

Xander felt a tightness growing in his chest as he climbed the few porch steps. He had returned to the house to angrily confront his family about their lies. Knowing the truth and knowing the danger it represented, he suddenly found an uncanny bond with the parents that had tried so hard to keep him protected from the truth.

"I'm sorry," he sobbed as he reached the porch.

His father shook his head before wrapping his arms tightly around Xander's back. Xander buried his face in his father's shoulder. He felt his mother's arm wrap around his back and she joined the two men.

When they finally broke their hug, his father wiped his eyes. "All I ever wanted was to keep you from this life. This," he said, gesturing to the scorched and smoking ground in the park, "it's just the beginning for you. Promise me something, Xander. Promise me you won't let it consume your life. You deserve so much more than spending the rest of your life being a Wind Warrior."

He placed his hand on his father's shoulder. He wanted to say something reassuring but couldn't find the words. In the end, Xander settled for a simple nod of his head.

He embraced his parents again, fighting against the strange sinking sensation in his gut. Their farewell seemed far too final for his liking.

"I'll see you guys again soon," Xander said but his words felt hollow even as he said them.

He could see his parents' reservations reflected in their eyes as he spoke. They didn't seem any more certain of his words than he did.

"We have to go," his grandfather said from the base of the steps.

Xander half turned toward the older man. In the distance, he could hear the sirens of approaching police and fire vehicles. He was far more concerned about the sounds he wouldn't hear, like the Fire Warriors returning to finish what they began.

With a sigh, Xander turned back to his parents and embraced them one last time.

"You can come with us, you know," he whispered into his father's ear.

His father shook his head. "Our lives are here now. The world you're going into has no place for normal people like us."

As they broke their hug, Xander turned toward the stairs. His mother clung to his hand a second longer before regrettably letting him go. Xander took the steps quickly and joined his awaiting grandfather.

"Take good care of him," his father said reproachfully to his grandfather. "You keep him safe."

To Xander's surprise, his grandfather didn't offer a scathing retort but instead nodded in agreement.

The pair of Wind Warriors walked away, turning down the street that led back to the park. Xander stole a glance over his shoulder and saw his mother leaning heavily against his father's shoulder.

"I'm worried about them," Xander said.

"I know," his grandfather conceded. "I am too. I'm going to have another warrior come watch them for a while, just until I'm sure the Fire Caste is going to leave them be."

He stole one last glance over his shoulder and thought about all he was sacrificing by leaving. He wasn't sure he'd ever see his parents again. Jessica, for all her faults, had been a close friend for years. He wouldn't have the chance to say goodbye to Sean, who had been his quirky best friend since they were children. All he could do now was pray that they remained safe long after he left.

"They'll be safe," his grandfather said, as though reading his thoughts.

"I know," Xander said. "I just get the feeling I'll never see them again."

His grandfather sighed. "I hope you're wrong—I really do."

CHAPTER 8

Xander held his breath as he and his grandfather flew over the puffy white clouds. The dense gust of air that carried them felt like traveling on a pillow. While the ride itself was comfortable, the fact that it didn't appear that anything was holding them aloft left Xander feeling highly unnerved.

They passed quickly through the air. The wind stung Xander's eyes, causing tears to streak down his cheeks. From the intermittent breaks in the clouds, he could see mountains giving way to wide expansive plains. In the distance, far beyond where the plains ended, rivers merged into a giant river delta that fed into the ocean.

The pair passed the time in forced silence. Neither had the urge to speak—not after their recent attack at the hands of the Fire Warriors. His grandfather's throat still bore the scorched finger marks from where he had been held. Even had they wanted to talk, however, it would have been impossible. Every word was stolen by the roaring wind as soon as it left their mouths.

Xander used the time to retreat into his thoughts. Despite being angry at her betrayal, his thoughts invariably fell back to Sammy. He had seen the handiwork of the Fire Warriors firsthand and knew the ruthlessness that they would use to get what they wanted. Logically, he knew that he should have killed her in the house when he had the chance. Logic, however, lost time and again to the strong emotions running through his heart. The connection he had felt for Sammy could easily be explained away as the connection they shared between the elements. It would have been easy to tell himself that it wasn't love that drew him to her—it was the evolution of the elements from wind to fire. He was made to fuel her power, which is why he was inexplicably drawn to her time and again.

Even if it made sense, Xander didn't believe that explanation. From the first moment he had looked into her eyes, he knew that she was someone unique. To lose her meant to lose his heart forever. He knew that's why he took her betrayal so badly. Before him was a woman he wasn't sure he wanted to live without, even after knowing her for only a week. Yet her first instinct when they were alone was to try to burn him, to kill him, so that her kind could claim their rightful place as the prime element.

It all sounded so crazy in his mind. Strangely, the thought that he had a deep spiritual connection with Sammy was the least crazy thing in his life. The fact that he so openly thought in terms of 'prime elements' and 'wind fueling fire' was why he was concerned for his sanity. Never mind the fact that he was currently flying through the air at an insane speed, all thanks to the special powers of his geriatric grandfather.

He hadn't been happy in school, but it had been a way to put off planning for his future. Now, he would have given anything to go back to being the oblivious college student, dating an annoying sorority girl, and hanging out with his geeky best friend.

Thinking of Sean made him almost as sad as thinking of his parents. At least his parents would understand why he had to leave. For Sean, Xander would just be there one day and be gone the next. He'd hear the stories about a wildfire in the city park and the rumors of a tornado touching down and he'd make assumptions, but never really know the truth.

His grandfather tapped him on the shoulder, pulling him from his revelry. He pointed below them, where the cloud cover had cleared and the crystal blue ocean sparkled in the moonlight. He knew the ocean was over six hundred miles away from White Halls and wondered again just how fast they were flying.

Xander wanted to ask where they were going but knew the attempt was futile. He would have to be patient, which clearly wasn't one of his strongest attributes.

He wasn't entirely sure if he fell asleep—or if his mind just began daydreaming to pass the time during the long flight—but Xander was startled by another impatient tap on his arm.

He followed his grandfather's gaze out ahead of their flight path and his eyes widened in awe and fear.

From the depths of the ocean, a massive waterspout sprang high into the air. The swirling water was a cyclone formed over the ocean, sucking up the salty water into a funnel reaching above the clouds. The power of the waterspout was remarkable and stole his breath.

Had Xander ever bothered with a bucket list, he would certainly have been able to mark this experience from the list.

He expected that they would fly past and continue on the way to their destination. When his grandfather didn't veer away from the mile-wide waterspout, Xander began tapping his shoulder impatiently. His grandfather brushed away his impertinent complaining and continued forward.

Xander's tapping quickly became a fervent shaking, against which his grandfather lashed out and knocked his hand aside.

The pair sped up as they approached the edge of the cyclone. Xander could smell the salty air mixed with an aromatic scent of fresh fish. The sea spray from the waterspout coated his face and soaked his clothes as they flew even closer. A much louder and more violent roar of the devastating swirling waves replaced the roar in his ears from flying—a sound to which he had grown accustomed.

Xander screamed despite himself as the duo crashed into the wave. He expected to be buffeted by the spinning water but was pleasantly surprised when he wasn't. Daring to open the eyes he hadn't even realized he closed, Xander saw a small bubble of air surrounding them as they passed through the water unfettered.

The trip through the cyclone was much quicker than Xander would have estimated. They emerged into the eye of the storm, a pillar of still air that opened to an incredible view of the stars above. The sound of the waterspout was greatly diminished in the eye as was the torrential winds.

The pair slowed considerable in the eye and began drifting downward. Xander stole a glance past his descending feet and was stunned by what rose to meet them.

In the eye of the waterspout, hovering above the choppy sea waves, an island floated in the air. The surface of the island was unnaturally flat and a giant marble keep rested on its top. Large pillars rose up to meet sloping rooftops. Ornate steps led down to flowering gardens. Mosaics were intricately designed into the walkways connecting the multitude of outlying buildings.

As they touched down in the center courtyard of the keep, a group of men and women emerged from the buildings to meet them. They were all similarly dressed in white shirts, pants, and sandals that reminded Xander reminiscently of a modernized-ancient Greek culture.

None of the men and women in the group was younger than their mid-forties. For once, Xander felt horribly out of place, like a volunteer in an old folk's home during Bingo night.

He smiled sheepishly and waved to them as they approached.

"Hi," he said and was surprised that he could hear himself within the waterspout. He had no doubt that this remarkable feat was their doing.

The gathered group smiled broadly at him, though Xander suspected most of their affection was directed toward his grandfather. Their gazes told of a great reverence to the old man.

"Everyone, I'd like you to meet my grandson and

the newest Wind Warrior, Xander Sirocco."

His grandfather turned toward Xander with a more confident smile than he remembered seeing on the elder man before.

"Xander, I'd like to introduce you to your aunts and uncles. They're going to teach you how to be a legend."

CHAPTER 9

Near the foothills of the Rocky Mountains, somewhere outside Los Angeles, California, a small crevice led deep into the earth. No wider than a man, the small chasm belched soot and foul-smelling sulfur into the air.

Residents who lived nearby had complained to environmental organizations when the rift appeared a few months earlier but no one had yet been able to make it far inside. The heat within the crevice was intense. The residents were told that it was probably a result of tectonic shifting along a fault line and that it was a flume leading to an underground magma pocket.

The chasm led further into the earth than the environmental organizations believed. Beyond the entrance of the cavern was a dizzying series of natural and unnatural caverns leading deep into the earth. Natural lava tubes merged into carved stone tunnels that transitioned into rough chambers filled with a multitude of stalagmites and stalactites.

Beyond the furthest of these expansive chambers, the passages all became worked stone. Like the story of all roads leading to Rome, the carven passages all led to a massive central chamber. In its depths, lava flowed freely in a blistering swirl that caused the air throughout the rounded room to dance in the heat.

Hovering above the lava, suspended by a latticework of catwalks and support pillars, a gargantuan dark stone castle rose from its charred island.

Pale-skinned men and women, the only color on their skin coming from the ashy soot that settled on their bodies, crossed the catwalks and entered the castle.

In the heart of the castle stood an obsidian throne, on which sat Lord Balor. The tall man leaned back against the chair, his dark hair cascading over his shoulders in waves. His body was draped in crimson and black clothes that clung to him in the oppressive heat. His body was soaked in sweat, adding to his sour disposition.

A Fire Warrior stepped through the throne-room doors and hurried to the Lord's side. Leaning close, he whispered into Lord Balor's ear.

"My lord, Lady Sammy and her warriors have returned from their mission."

"And?" he asked, his voice echoing in the long chamber.

The warrior shook his head. Lord Balor dismissed him with a wave before clenching the arms of his chair in anger.

"Send her in," he ordered. The warrior with whom he'd been speaking before the messenger interrupted them stepped to Lord Balor's side.

Sammy entered with a small entourage of Fire Warriors behind her. Her silky dress from the spring formal was gone, replaced by black leather pants and half-jacket. A similarly short shirt clung to her body beneath the jacket, exposing her midriff.

The group approached the throne and stopped at the base of the steps. As a group, they bowed before their Lord.

"We've returned, Lord Balor," Sammy said. Her nervousness was evident in her tone.

She raised her head and looked at the pair of intimidating Fire Warriors on the raised throne dais. Lord Balor towered over the other Fire Warriors. His size and fighting prowess combined to solidify his place as Lord over their offshoot clan.

Sammy knew that not all the Fire Caste agreed with Lord Balor's plans to assassinate the remaining Wind Warriors but none dared speak against him for fear a violent reprisal.

The man beside Lord Balor lacked the physical stature but scared her far worse. General Abraxas was virtually unparalleled in his fighting skill and ruthlessness in battle. Their clan had already lost a number of Fire Warriors just because of Abraxas' displeasure.

"Did you succeed in locating the new Wind Warrior?" Lord Balor asked. Sammy knew he was leading her into a verbal trap but she dared not defy him or lie to him.

"We did, my Lord."

"And is he dead?" The words were laced with a barely veiled threat.

"N-no, my Lord," Sammy stuttered. She closed her eyes and tensed in anticipation of his retribution. "But I have left men in his town. We will succeed…"

Lord Balor opened his hand and a jet of searing

white flame flew from his palm. The fire engulfed the Fire Warrior kneeling beside Sammy. The man screamed in anguish but the yell was short-lived. The heat from the flame turned him to ash almost instantaneously.

Sammy felt the waves of heat rolling over her and felt her hair threaten to ignite from the onslaught. She clenched her jaw tightly and bore the pain the heat caused on her exposed flesh.

When the punishment was done and the warrior burned to black ash, Lord Balor dismissed the flame.

"I won't accept failure," he stated angrily. "Were it not for the fact that you are my daughter, it would have been you I burned today."

Sammy nodded. "Yes… Father."

Lord Balor waved his hand and dismissed the rest of the Fire Warriors. "I wish to speak to my daughter alone."

Sammy looked up as the booted feet of the other warriors quickly retreated from the chamber. General Abraxas still stood at his place of honor beside her father.

"Tell me of this new Wind Warrior."

She swallowed hard, her throat parched from the heat. As much as she loathed lying to her father for fear of his reprisal, she knew she couldn't tell him the whole truth. She couldn't tell him that she had thought about him every night since meeting him. She couldn't tell him that she hated herself for betraying him. She couldn't tell him that she had cried herself to sleep that night after the spring formal and about how she longed to run back to him that very night and apologize profusely.

Sammy had never been anything other than a

brashly independent woman but the connection she felt with Xander was far beyond anything she understood.

"He's new to his powers," she explained. "He's still trying to figure them out but he's a quick learner."

"And yet he defeated you," General Abraxas hissed. His voice was like a serpent, sliding between his sharpened teeth.0

"I wasn't prepared for his level of skill. I'd be better prepared if we met again."

"I'm glad to hear you say that, my daughter. You're going to have another chance to redeem yourself. You're going to return to the surface and find this Wind Warrior. And this time, you won't fail me."

Sammy's heart pounded in her chest. It was more than she could have hoped for. Her father was going to send her back to Xander, completely unaware that she couldn't harm him if she wanted to.

"And to make sure you don't fail me again, you'll be accompanied by General Abraxas. He will ensure the Wind Warrior dies this time."

Her breath froze in her throat. Abraxas was ruthless and unstoppable. There was no way Xander could survive against him.

"Is that absolutely necessary, Father?" she asked. "This new warrior is little more than a child. He doesn't pose a threat to us. I expected him to be like you always described the Wind Caste to be: violent, unstable, and dangerous. He wasn't any of these things. Couldn't we just—?"

"Silence!" Lord Balor yelled. The room seemed to shake in response to his rage. "You will find this boy and this time you won't come home until you succeed."

General Abraxas smiled wickedly, his sharpened teeth glistening in the torchlight. He leaned dangerously forward from his place beside the throne. "And this time when you two meet, you'll make sure that either he dies… or you do."

Lord Balor shot an angry glance at his general before returning his glance to his daughter. "Don't fail us again."

"Yes, Lord Balor," she replied sheepishly. Tears stung her eyes and she kept her head lowered so her hair concealed her face. Her heart ached and her stomach twisted itself in knots. She didn't know how to save Xander, especially from someone as maniacal as Abraxas. If there was a way, however, she knew she'd figure it out. Somehow.

The large throne room doors swung shut as Sammy left. General Abraxas took a step down from the raised dais and stood before Lord Balor. The bald General ran a hand over his sweaty scalp and exposed his rows of filed teeth.

"She's going to be trouble," he told the Lord.

Lord Balor's stern gaze remained on the closed door as though he didn't hear Abraxas speak.

"When the time comes, she won't do it," he continued unabashed by Balor's seeming indifference. "She has feelings for the Wind Warrior. She won't be able to kill him."

"Then you'll do it yourself," Lord Balor said

finally as he rubbed his chin thoughtfully. "That should be the only thing that concerns you right now. Leave my daughter to me."

"If she fails, our master won't be happy."

Lord Balor slammed his gauntleted fist down onto the arm of the throne. The sound exploded into the large room, echoing around its vaulted ceiling.

"Don't you dare lecture me on the will of our master!" he bellowed. "And don't you ever threaten my daughter again. Need I remind you of our master's plans for her?"

General Abraxas bowed apologetically. "Forgive me, my Lord. I haven't forgotten our master's plans. Perhaps I overstepped my bounds. I meant only that Sammy walks a dangerous path."

"Then it's your job to keep her safe, Abraxas. Our master won't accept any harm coming to her."

Lord Balor stood from his throne and walked around behind the raised dais. He brushed aside one of the hanging tapestries, revealing the stonework wall behind it. He ran his fingers along the wall until they found a small, recessed gray stone amidst a sea of others. A grinding noise filled the room as he pressed the innocuous stone. The rest of the stonework before Lord Balor parted, revealing a secret passage that led deeper into the volcanic cavern. Heat far more intense than that within the throne room washed over the pair of Fire Warriors as they stood at the precipice.

He turned away from the opening and faced the General again. "You told my daughter that either the Wind Warrior dies or she would. I make you the same promise, General. If any harm comes to Sammy, I will give you a quick death, which is more than our master would grant you. Keep her safe or don't bother coming back."

General Abraxas bowed again, though his expression held nothing but contempt for the Lord.

Lord Abraxas stepped through the secret passage and the stonework closed behind him.

Abraxas dropped the pretense of piety and walked back to the dais. He climbed its narrow steps before turning toward the empty room. With a flourish, he collapsed into the hard throne. A wicked smile spread across his lips as he surveyed the room and imagined the Fire Caste prostrate before him in reverence.

Sammy watched through the narrow crack between the throne room doors. Her eyes widened as her father disappeared through the hidden doorway behind the hanging tapestry. Even from the great distance, she could practically see General Abraxas' contemptuous snarl as the warrior took his seat on Lord Balor's throne.

Ignoring the General, her gaze fell back onto the tapestry that now concealed the secret opening in the rock. She had lived in the castle for nineteen years, leaving only in her attempt to kill Xander, and yet had never seen that opening before. Whatever lay beyond, Sammy felt irrevocably drawn to it. It pulled on her in much the same way Xander had when they first met. It was a surreal feeling, as though forces outside her and beyond her control were pulling her through her own life like a marionette.

"What are you doing there?" a Fire Warrior guard asked as he approached her from behind.

Startled, Sammy spun quickly toward the man. When the guard realized he was addressing the daughter of Lord Balor, he quickly averted his eyes and his stern expression softened.

"Forgive me, Lady Balor. I didn't realize it was you."

Sammy cleared her throat, uncomfortable with being addressed as part of the Fire Caste royalty.

"What can I do for you?" she asked, her mind drifting again to the secret passage and whatever lay beyond.

"I was ordered to escort you to your quarters."

Sammy looked longingly over her shoulder toward the crack between the doors before sighing. She nodded wordlessly and followed the guard away from the throne room doors.

CHAPTER 10

The wail of fire sirens split the silent night's air. Sean pulled back the apartment's curtains and looked outside. In the distance, flickering flames illuminated the relatively dark town. The swirling red, white, and blue of fire trucks and police cars converged on the scene in a dense roar of sirens. As he watched, another fire truck rushed past his apartment complex.

A knot formed in the pit of his stomach as he looked out the window. The fire was clearly coming from the area of town in which Xander lived. With everything else happening to his best friend, it didn't seem at all far-fetched to believe that Xander was somehow involved.

He pulled his cell phone out of his pocket and dialed the number again. The phone rang over and over with no answer. Finally, the voice mail picked up with an automated tone.

"You've reached Xander," it said. "I can't come to the phone right now. Leave a message and I'll call you back."

Sean swallowed hard as his eyes fell on the firefighters battling the visible blaze. Sighing, Sean waited patiently for the beep.

"Hey Xander. This is message number forty-six

or so. Where are you? Give me a call when you get this."

He hung up the cell phone and slid it into his pocket. Sean let the curtain fall back into place and he turned, sitting heavily onto the worn couch. His gaze drifted to the mound of clothes and college textbooks piled on the edge of the couch. Xander's backpack was still discarded on the floor, in the last place it had been left before he disappeared.

At first, Sean had enviously assumed that Xander had gone home with Sammy after the spring formal. The fire, however, changed that. Seeing its budding beginning had been enough to send Sean's mind down a dark path, one that assumed his best friend was in grave danger. The fact that Xander wouldn't answer his phone only added to his growing fear.

Sean felt a nervousness building in his ample gut. It wasn't like Xander to disappear. If there was one thing about his best friend, the man was unerringly predictable. That was before his powers appeared, Sean had to remind himself.

He pulled out his cell phone once again and looked at the time. It was already past midnight and most of White Halls was sound asleep. Sean looked down the narrow hallway leading from the living room and saw his own bedroom door, still sitting partially open. His bed was inviting, and his body was certainly tired enough to sleep, but his mind was still blazing with concern. He knew that trying to sleep would be a wasted effort.

Instead, Sean picked up his keys from the coffee table and walked toward the front door. It might be late but he couldn't go to sleep until he knew what was happening. If Xander wasn't at the apartment, there was only one other place Sean imagined he would have gone. If Xander's parents didn't know where he was, then Sean would truly worry.

He hurried down the narrow steps of the apartment and let the small bell above the door jingle as he walked outside. The parking lot was full and dark; only a single lamppost illuminated the area and it resided on the far side from where he had parked. Had it not been for the insanely low crime rate in White Halls, Sean might have been concerned. As it was, he walked to his car with barely a glance upward.

He slipped behind the wheel of his car and started the engine with a loud sputter. A noxious cloud of black smoke that shot out of the tailpipe accompanied the rattling engine. The smell within the car quickly became atrocious and Sean rolled down his window as he backed out of his parking spot.

He put on his turn signal and prepared to ease onto the traffic-less road. He was so engrossed with checking on Xander that he never noticed the blonde-haired man watching his apartment from the deep shadows across the street. As Sean pulled away from the apartment building, the man stretched his fingers wide and a small flame erupted in his hand.

White Halls was hardly big enough to necessitate a long drive. He could have just as easily walked the mile and a half to Xander's house but it wasn't Sean's style to walk when there was a perfectly capable car handy.

As he turned onto Xander's street, his vision filled with the twirling lights from atop a sea of police cars and fire trucks. Firemen in gasmasks dragged hoses across the narrow street and sprayed pressurized jets of water into smoldering trees and bushes.

The once vibrant green grass of the park was scorched and charred, leaving the ruined ground exposed beneath. Rivers of water rushed down either side of the street and poured like an angry waterfall into the narrow metal drains. The ground was muddy and large pools of water still soaked the grassy field.

"What did you get into, Xander?" Sean muttered.

With a renewed sense of urgency, Sean tried driving down the street. As he approached, a police officer stepped in front of his car and shined a flashlight through the windshield. Sean squinted and raised a hand to block the light. As soon as he had come to a complete stop, the officer approached his open window.

"Did you see all the emergency vehicles?" the officer asked, gesturing to the haphazardly parked cars. "You can't drive through here."

Sean looked past the officer. He could practically see Xander's house from where he was stopped. "I just need to get to my friend's house. It's right down the street."

The officer shook his head. "You can't drive over these hoses. You can park back here and walk down there, if you need to. Just stay away from the firefighters while they're working."

Sean begrudgingly parked his car against the curb. The scene was controlled chaos as he skirted across the far side of the road. He did his best to avoid the thick hoses attached to the fire hydrants he passed but generally kept his head down as he passed the scene, as though the police would be able to tell just by looking at him that he had a relationship to one of the men involved in the fire.

Xander's car was parked in the driveway as Sean approached but the house itself was dark. No light bled through from the kitchen or dining room. There wasn't even the typical flickering glow from the television, which Xander's grandfather watched fairly religiously.

As he climbed the steps, he sidestepped piles of dirt and soot that coated both the edges of the stairs and the porch landing in front of the door. The scene only reignited Sean's concern for his best friend. Reaching out cautiously, he knocked on the door.

For a long minute, he stood on the porch waiting for someone to come answer. When he didn't hear any movement inside, he rang the doorbell as well.

Sean turned his back to the front of the house while he waited and looked out over the street. The other houses in the neighborhood were equally quiet, though he could see lights glowing through a few of the windows.

Sighing—his fears not abated, as he would have hoped—Sean started to walk back down the stairs before he heard the door handle behind him turn. He quickly turned back toward Xander's house as the door opened a crack. Despite the gloom within the house, he could see Xander's father staring out at him.

"Mr. Sirocco?" Sean said. The man looked horribly aged. His eyes looked sunken and his skin had an oily texture that looked like he was unwashed.

"Sean," Xander's father said. His voice was slightly hoarse as though thick with emotion. "Xander's not here."

Sean felt taken aback by his bluntness. "Do you know where he is? I've been trying to call him but he's not answering. He left some stuff at my place."

"He went out of town with his grandfather for a while," Mr. Sirocco replied quickly. "I'll have him give you a call when he gets back in town."

Xander's father tried to hastily close the door behind him but Sean stuck out his foot and blocked it from closing completely. He grimaced as the door slammed against his foot. Looking exasperated, Xander's father opened the door a little wider again.

"Sean…"

"Can you at least tell me where he went? Something strange is going on."

The elder man's expression softened as he looked at Xander's longtime friend. "Sean, the best thing you can do is leave it all alone for a while. I know you're worried but there's nothing you can do for Xander right now. Go home. Go back to school. Go on with your life and I promise that if Xander comes back, I'll make sure he calls you."

"If?" Sean said suddenly. "If he comes back?"

"Go home, Sean," Xander's father repeated more sternly.

Crestfallen, Sean turned away from the door and took a few hitched paces down the steep steps. He expected to hear the door slam behind him but instead he heard a telltale creak as it opened slightly wider.

"Sean."

He turned and saw Mr. Sirocco standing half out of the door. The older man looked around nervously before his attention fell back to Sean.

"Sir?"

"I know you don't know what's going on right now. And I'm really glad that Xander has such a good friend as you. Just… just be careful out there right now. I know this sounds like elementary school advice but don't talk to strangers. There are some dangerous people in town right now."

-"Do they have to do with Xander? Are they why he had to leave?"

"Goodbye, Sean."

The door shut solidly behind Xander's father as the man disappeared back into the enveloping darkness of the interior. Sean shook his head and turned back toward his car. This trip was supposed to put his mind at ease. If anything, he was even more nervous now than he had been when he thought Xander had just slept over at Sammy's house.

The fires in the park seemed mostly under control by the time Sean reached the sidewalk in front of the house. Firefighters were busy rolling up hoses and a number of the vehicles had already pulled away. Their absence gave Sean the chills. He hadn't realized how much the police at the end of the street had set his mind at ease, especially with Xander's father's cryptic warning about dangerous strangers in White Halls. As the last of the trucks were getting ready to depart, the street suddenly seemed eerily quiet, as though all the other residents on the street had closed proverbial shutters and pulled their curtains just a little tighter against the windows.

Sean pulled his jacket tight around his body, trying to ward off a chill that was coming from within. He lowered his head and hurried toward his car, hoping to reach it before the last fire trucks left. To his dismay, the firefighters loaded their hoses and climbed into the cabs while he was still about a block away. They pulled away hurriedly, leaving him in the disturbing night's gloom.

"Excuse me," a voice said softly behind him.

Sean clutched his chest and turned, holding his other hand up defensively in front of his face. A man seemed to materialize behind him as he emerged from the deep shadows. The stranger's blonde hair glistened in the faint moonlight but the rest of his body was swaddled in dark clothes that looked almost like leather. The man held his arms behind his back and smiled—but he looked like a stereotypical vampire, eagerly awaiting his next meal.

"It's awfully late to be walking the streets," the man said.

Sean couldn't place the odd accent but it clearly sounded like English was the man's second language.

"I could say the same thing to you," Sean replied.

The man chuckled to himself before looking over his shoulder, toward Xander's house. "I noticed you just came from the Sirocco residence. What did you talk about?"

"Listen buddy. I don't know you and we're not having this conversation." Sean hoped his false bravado was good enough to fool the stranger.

The man's smile vanished from his face. "Tell me where I can find Xander Sirocco."

"Never heard of him," Sean replied, swallowing hard.

The man clucked his tongue disapprovingly. "I can make this difficult for you, if that's what you want. Either way, you're going to tell me what I want to know."

Sean glanced around nervously, hoping some concerned citizen would suddenly appear and rescue him. The houses around him remained dark, though, and no one seemed likely to save him.

The man withdrew a hand from behind his back. His palm seemed to glow with an inner light. It radiated heat and the smell of sulfur washed over Sean.

"This is your last chance before we make this harder than it needs to be. Tell me what you talked about! Tell me where I can find the Wind Warrior!"

Sean glanced suddenly over the stranger's shoulder and his eyes widened in surprise. The Fire Warrior followed Sean's gaze and he turned to look at what approached from behind him. The area was completely empty, though. As the Fire Warrior turned back angrily toward Sean—upset at the obvious ruse— Sean's punch caught him across the jaw.

The Fire Warrior staggered before dropping painfully onto his back. Sean immediately clenched his hand and shook it.

"Ow!" he yelled into the night air. "Man, that hurts. Who knew doing that hurt so bad?"

The Fire Warrior shook his head and blinked

heavily as he cleared his vision. Seeing the man recovering, Sean turned and ran toward his car. He huffed as he hurried across the street and was soon reminded of the myriad of reasons he hated running. He realized, however, that he always said the only way he'd be caught dead running was if someone was chasing him.

He reached the far sidewalk and turned toward his car when a ball of flame went flying by his head, missing him by inches. He felt his hairs curl from the heat, withdrawing from the scorching fireball. The flame struck his windshield and exploded in a shower of sparks. The fire quickly caught on his hood and on his worn fabric interior. Within moments, the car was consumed in flames.

Sean turned nervously toward the stranger. Another ball of flames started growing between the hands of the advancing man. The previous smile on the Fire Warrior's face had become a snarl of rage.

Turning again, Sean ran into the yard next to him, dodging between the young trees that dotted the landscape. White Halls' main crossroad ran parallel to Xander's road, which meant that if he made it through just a couple of interconnected yards, he would reach the main road and, hopefully, flag down a passing car.

The yard he ran through wasn't fenced and bled seamlessly into the rear of the next yard. Despite the strain in his chest from his heavy breathing, Sean picked up his knees and pushed himself forward.

The world behind him lit up as a ball of flames struck the muddy ground. He could feel the intense waves of heat and saw the sparks settle on the grass around him but he didn't dare slow or even look behind him.

Sean ran past the next house but frowned as he approached the road. The house had a tall, privacy hedgerow separating it from the road. He couldn't see the cars passing, nor could they see him. More importantly, he would have to push through the hedge before he could get to the relative safety of the road.

Lowering his head, Sean slammed into the hedge. His weight drove the branches aside. They scratched at his skin and pulled on his clothing as he pushed forward. Despite the burning in his legs, his biggest fear was stopping halfway through the hedge and being exposed to the maniac chasing him.

To his relief, the hedge finally gave way and he saw the cool night's sky over the street beyond. As he took a step out of the hedge, his foot caught on the smashed branches. His shoe came cleanly off his foot and he staggered out and into the street.

Sean looked up as headlights fell over him. He could hear the screeching of tires as he threw his hands up in front of his face and closed his eyes. For a long moment, he waited for the inevitable impact. Slowly, as he realized he hadn't been hit, he stole a glance through a narrowly opened eyelid.

The car had stopped just a few inches away from him.

With a sigh of relief, Sean hobbled around to the passenger's side of the car. He threw open the door and slid inside without caring who was behind the wheel or where they were going.

"Thank you, thank you," he gushed. "You really

saved my…"

His words froze in his throat as he looked over to the driver. Jessica frown deepened as her eyes grew dangerously narrow.

"No," she said angrily. "No, no, no. Absolutely not. Get out of my car, Sean."

"Any other time, I would. Trust me. But now, I just need you to drive!"

She let go of the steering wheel and shoved against his considerable weight, trying to force him out of the partially opened car door.

"Get out of my car, Sean! I'm not joking with you. Get out!"

Sean was forced to grab hold of the handle above the door as a last ditch effort to keep from being forced out of the car. For a thin woman, Jessica wielded considerable strength when she was angry.

"Get out!"

"Stop pushing me," Sean yelled.

The Fire Warrior burst through the hedgerow and staggered out in front of the car. He turned his gaze to the arguing occupants and the sneer returned to his face.

"There you are!" the warrior bellowed as he leaned on the hood of Jessica's car. "No more running. Tell me what I want to know!"

"What is wrong with you people?" she screamed. "Get off of my car, you freak!"

She stopped pushing Sean long enough to slam her hand down on the car's horn. The roar of the horn overwhelmed the loud, three-way conversation.

Startled, the Fire Warrior staggered off the hood and looked in horror at the vehicle. He stretched his hands above his head and they began to glow white-hot. Flames licked his fingertips seconds before he slammed them down on Jessica's hood.

The fire spread across the hood and rolled up over the windshield, blinding Jessica and Sean to what lay beyond the front of the car.

In a panic, Jessica screamed and stomped down on the accelerator. The car leapt forward and they both heard an unpleasant thud as the car sped away.

Blinded, they swerved from side to side across the road. Sean leaned out of his partially opened door and saw them coming up quickly to an intersection.

"Stop, Jessica," he said as calmly as his nervous body would allow. He could see them still accelerating dangerously, so he reached over and placed a hand on her arm. "Stop the car, Jessica."

She released the gas pedal and slammed down instead on the brake. Sean jerked forward and his forehead struck the edge of the doorframe. He rocked backward as the car came to a stop and grabbed his head.

"Gah!" he yelled, actual words eluding him.

Jessica's chest heaved as she struggled for breath. Her hands were clenched tightly around the steering wheel so tightly that her knuckles practically glowed white. As they sat in the car—Jessica clutching the wheel silently and Sean clutching his head and groaning—the flames flickered down and died away on the hood of the car. Only a layer of soot remained over the windshield, blurring, but not obscuring, their vision.

"Did I hit him?" Jessica squeaked in a nearly inaudible voice. "It sounded like I hit him."

Sean groaned and leaned his head back against the headrest. "If you did, good for you."

Her cheeks went from a pale white to a flushed angry in the span of a breath. "This is all your fault!"

Sean opened one eye and immediately regretted the movement as another stab of pain rolled through his head. "I think I have a concussion."

"I don't care! I hit a guy with my car! Do you even know what this means?"

"You really are a man-killer?"

She let go of the steering wheel and shoved against Sean's body again. "That's it! Get out of my car! I'm serious this time!"

Begrudgingly, Sean stepped gingerly out of the still-open door. Every movement made his head scream in pain. He leaned down and looked apologetically at Jessica.

She shot him a glance that fully expressed her feelings. "Close the door and get away from my car. You've done enough damage already."

Sean closed the door and looked through the open window. "I really am sorry about this, if it makes a difference."

"It doesn't, Sean. Don't ever talk to me again!"

She drove quickly away, leaving Sean standing abandoned in the middle of the road. He stole a glance behind him but he couldn't see the Fire Warrior.

Suddenly realizing just how exposed he was in the middle of the road, he turned toward his apartment building and jogged slowly away.

CHAPTER 11

"These," his grandfather explained, "are you aunts and uncles."

Four middle-aged men and women stood on the tiled mosaic on which Xander and his grandfather had landed. They looked as different from one another as they did from him and he doubted they were truly related by anything more than the power that coursed through them all.

"Hi," he offered weakly.

A long-haired man stepped forward. His black hair was pulled back into a loose ponytail from which wisps of hair escaped. Xander extended his hand to shake but the man brushed his hand aside and embraced him in a massive hug.

"My name is Giovanni," the Wind Warrior said, his thick Italian accent making him hard to understand. His words came out in a broken cadence that told Xander that English wasn't his first language. "We have been waiting for you for a long time. Welcome."

Xander smiled at the warm welcome. In turn, he was introduced to the three others. A tall, muscular woman was introduced as Aunt Thea. Her posture and graceful movements left Xander feeling intimidated in her presence.

The other woman was Alicia. She seemed far more the doting grandmother type than dangerous warrior. She flashed a disarming smile as she hugged him.

The final man was introduced as Uncle Patrick. His flaming red hair matched his fiery personality. Instead of a hug from the enthusiastic Irishman, Xander was punched playfully in the shoulder.

As they resumed their places around him, Xander had the chance to look at the gathered group. His smile faded slowly and sadness crept into his eyes.

"Is something wrong, dear?" Alicia asked. Xander wasn't entirely sure if she would pinch his cheeks or offer him cookies if he seemed upset.

"I just expected more of you," he said.

His heart felt heavy. Just the small group of Fire Warriors that ambushed him and his grandfather greatly outnumbered the small group sitting on the floating island.

"This isn't everyone," his grandfather said, placing a comforting hand on his shoulder. "There are two more of us."

Xander frowned. "Just two more?"

"I warned you that we were a dying breed. You don't know how much it means to see a young Wind Warrior joining our ranks."

"So where are the other two?"

Giovanni jerked a thumb over his shoulder. Xander followed the gesture to the domed marble building that sat in the center of the island. "Robert keeps the island afloat."

Xander turned slowly and admired the wall of water that was drawn upward by impossibly strong winds. "Just one man is doing all this?"

"We may be few," Thea said without humor, "but we're more than a match for a handful of Fire Warriors."

"Your Uncle Bart is watching your parents," his grandfather said.

Xander's heart fluttered with relief at the news. He hugged his grandfather, who groaned as Xander pushed against the minor burns on his chest and ribs.

"Thank you," Xander said.

"They're my family too. I didn't want to leave them, but I sure wouldn't leave them undefended. Bart will protect them for us."

Looking behind him, Xander noticed an outcropping of marble shaped haphazardly like a bench. He walked over and collapsed onto the seat.

"Is something the matter, lad?" Patrick asked.

Xander rubbed his hands together furiously, as though trying to remove a stubborn smudge of dirt.

"I appreciate you guys bringing me here and this place is amazing. It's just… there are so few of you. Even with the other two, there are only eight of us left? Against the entire Fire Caste?"

The aunts and uncles all exchanged nervous glances. His grandfather nodded solemnly and took a seat beside Xander. Xander knew this wasn't a conversation he was going to want to hear.

"I didn't bring you here to form an army. I brought you here to learn to control your powers, so you could reach your fullest potential as a Wind Warrior."

"They're going to destroy the planet," he pleaded. "How can you all just sit here and accept that?"

"Because it's the way it's supposed to be," Giovanni said as he came over and knelt before Xander. "You are young and, as you may have noticed, we are not."

The aunts and uncles laughed amongst themselves.

"We've had a lot of time to prepare for this. Before you came, we were ready to grow old and die, knowing that the reins had been passed to the Fire Caste. With you, it changes things. You're another chance for the last of the Wind Caste to make a difference in the world before we go."

"How can you be so calm about it?" Xander asked. Gone was the vitriol in his voice. He spoke instead with a quiet reservation.

"Because it doesn't matter if we like the next stage in the world's evolution," Thea replied. "We've done our job over the past few thousand years. Our kind has been the inspiration and the muses for humanity. We've breathed the life of creativity into their minds. We've helped them build skyscrapers that reach toward the heavens. We've helped them build planes that let them feel the wind in their faces. We've inspired them to fly to the stars. But our time is coming to an end and the Earth needs to be reborn. That's the role of the Fire Caste."

"But they're willing to kill us to get there," he said softly. He wasn't yet ready to accept the end of the world so easily.

"Aye," said Patrick, "and if it's a fight they want, then it's a fight they'll get. We'll accept the Fire Caste when we've all grown old and died but I'll be damned if we're going to let those greedy buggers kill us off before our time."

Xander smiled—glad to hear the fire still burned in the bellies of the other Wind Warriors. "Then train me."

"We will," Alicia said, again flashing her disarming maternal smile.

"Come," his grandfather said as he stood from the bench. "Let's get you cleaned up, changed, and, most importantly, rested. You're going to have a lot of work ahead of you."

That night, sleep refused to come. Despite the exhaustion he felt, Xander's mind swirled with hundreds of individual thoughts. He climbed up the stairs of his small, two-story marble cottage and opened the shutters, letting in the cool night's breeze. Within the flume of water, the roar was barely noticeable. It sounded like a distant waterfall, soothing and peaceful. In the heart of the hidden island, it was easy for him to forget that an entire army of supernatural people were trying to kill him.

Of all the thoughts flitting through his mind, the thoughts of Sammy emerged time and time again to the forefront. He should hate her, he knew, but he couldn't help but feel drawn to her.

Xander climbed out the window and onto the red clay shingled roof. His sandaled feet clicked against the shingles as he climbed toward the pinnacle of the house. Just short of the peak, Xander sat down and laid back. Far above his head, he could faintly see a circle of twinkling stars. He had often looked out the window of his home in White Halls and admired the stars on cool nights like this. On the island, however, there were virtually no lights. The painted strip of the Milky Way was framed behind the brightly glowing stars. Somehow, he knew that Sammy would have loved sharing this view with him.

He was so engrossed in his stargazing that he didn't realize someone else had arrived until he heard the click of feet stepping on the loose tiles.

Xander sat up hastily and began summoning an orb of air between his outstretched hands.

"Calm yourself," Uncle Giovanni laughed, his arms held out wide defensively. "It's just Uncle Giovanni."

Xander sighed and shook his head. Giovanni had scared him nearly to death, which was exactly what he didn't need after the past couple days.

"Can I sit?"

Xander nodded and the Italian took a seat beside him. For a long moment, he didn't say a word. Giovanni craned his neck backward and enjoyed the same stars that Xander was admiring.

"I used to come up on the rooftop too, when I was younger. But when I was younger, I came up here usually to get away from my brothers and sisters."

Xander looked over at the older man. "Did you have a lot of brothers and sisters?"

Giovanni laughed into the still night air. "We are Italian. Of course I had a lot of brothers and sisters!"

He smiled at the Italian. Like he had always felt with his grandfather, Xander instantly felt a connection with the man.

"What happened to them?" Xander asked hesitantly.

Giovanni waved a hand dismissively. "They passed away some time ago. We have many brothers and sisters because we don't live long enough. Too much good Italian food and wine."

"Were they all Wind Warriors?"

"Some. Not all. But we loved each other like we were all of the same caste."

Xander smiled at the man. He tilted his head back and stared back up at the stars. He couldn't imagine what it would be like to have a huge family, wrestling and joking together. There was a time when he really thought he wanted a family. Granted, Xander knew he was too young now but sometime when he was older, he could envision kids of his own. Of course, that seemed less and less likely now. Inexplicably, his thoughts drifted again to Sammy and a small smile spread across his face.

"What is her name?" Giovanni asked.

"Excuse me?"

"When a man comes out here on his own and stares up at the stars with a wistful smile on his face, he is always thinking of a woman, no?"

Xander blushed in the darkness. "Her name is Sammy."

"Sammy," the Italian said. "It's a good name. So tell me about this girl."

"It's complicated."

"So, make it simple for me,"

"She's a Fire Warrior."

Giovanni whistled into the night air. "Oh, yeah, that makes it complicated. It's a good thing you have me for a teacher."

Xander propped himself up on an elbow. "Why? What is it you're going to teach me?"

"First thing I will teach you is how to pick a better girl," Giovanni laughed. "But later, I teach you how to fly."

"You're going to teach me how to fly?" Xander asked, sitting straight up on the rooftop.

"Of course. How do you think I got onto the roof?"

Xander hadn't considered it before. He had just assumed that Giovanni had climbed out the window, like he had.

"Teach me now."

"About the girls or about the flying?"

Xander smiled. "The flying."

"Okay. Come to the edge of the roof."

Together, they cautiously slid down the sloped shingled roof until they were at the edge of the rooftop. Xander looked over the edge as he stood and realized the ground was a dizzying distance below. In the gloom of the night, he could barely make out the tall bushes below.

"So what do I do? Do I make a wind to keep me aloft? That seemed to be what my grandfather did."

"Sure, do that," Giovanni said.

The Italian shoved him from behind and Xander tumbled from the roof. He tried to focus on creating wind but his mind was gripped with panic as he fell head over feet. With a crash, he slammed into the bushes before landing hard on the ground.

Giovanni floated down to the ground and landed lithely beside him.

"How do you feel?"

Xander groaned. "Like I just got run over."

"It was a good start. We'll do better next time."

He pushed himself up until he was on his hands and knees. His ribs ached and his shoulder was bruised but he didn't seem to have any other injuries.

"What do I need to do different next time?"

Giovanni scratched his chin. "Next time? Focus less on falling and spend a little more time flying. Now, back to the roof."

Xander groaned as he walked back into the house and climbed the stairs back to the second floor.

CHAPTER 12

Sammy sat in one of the tall towers of the underground castle, staring out her narrow window. The cavern beyond was swelteringly hot. The heat rolled up the tower in waves. Each scorching pass stole the breath from her lungs and left her mouth dry.

Her room lacked any lights but it was strongly illuminated by the glow of the lava flow far below the castle's precipice. By the light of the flowing illumination, Sammy could see countless men and women moving hurriedly around the castle grounds. They were clad in dark leathers, their blonde hair—like Sammy's—was pulled back in functional buns and ponytails.

As she watched them from her tower, she was surprised by the overwhelming sense of sadness she felt for her fellow Fire Warriors. Only a select few had ever left their cavern, as Sammy had. Most lived their entire lives within the sweltering cave, awaiting the death of the last of the Wind Caste and their chance to rule the Earth. They had been told their entire lives that the Wind Warriors were evil; that it was their job to eliminate them to make way for the new elemental rule.

She felt sorry for them because they would

probably never have the chance to learn the truth as she had learned it. The Wind Caste wasn't evil, as she had been led to believe by her father and General Abraxas. Of course, that same misguided belief was evident in Xander as well. He judged all the Fire Caste by the actions of a few under General Abraxas' command. He had no idea the sheer number of Fire Caste that were dispersed throughout hundreds of underground castles just like this one.

Her heart ached at the thought of Xander. She had genuinely felt connected to him in a way she didn't think possible. The knowledge inside her throughout their short-lived relationship that she was going to betray him ate at her core. She wished she could see him again, at least under better circumstances than her pending mission with General Abraxas. He deserved to know the truth about how she felt and not just remember her for trying to kill him.

Sammy slid from her seat at the window and walked over to her bed. It barely yielded at all as she sat down. She stared around the barren room without really seeing the sparse and utilitarian decorations. Her mind was lost in its own memories as her eyes passed over the room.

She replayed her father's reproachful gaze in the throne room over and over in her mind; the way he callously killed one of her fellow warriors for the failure that she alone brought about. A sting of tears caused her to blink heavily in the smoky room. She blamed it on the soot in the air, something she had grown accustomed to living without over her month away. In her heart, though, she knew the truth.

A swift knock on the door was all that preceded Lord Balor as he opened the door and entered Sammy's room. She quickly wiped away the threatening tears and coughed politely to clear away any semblance of emotion that might remain when she spoke.

She quickly climbed to her feet in the presence of the castle's Lord.

"Sit," he ordered as he closed the door behind him.

Sammy did as she was told, taking her place back on the firm bed. Lord Balor retrieved the room's only chair and sat across from her.

They sat in silence as Sammy eagerly waited for her father to speak. It was unusual for him to visit her in her room. Most of their interactions were reserved for when she was kneeling before his throne.

Lord Balor cleared his throat and crossed his arms over his chest. "I don't think I need to tell you how disappointed I am at your failure. Your mission was instrumental in us assuming our reign of the Earth."

Sammy felt her ire rise in her chest. The father who had once been so doting and loving as she grew had become so incredibly distant recently. He spoke to her now as though she were a common warrior instead of his only child and heir to the throne.

"I can't have you fail me again. I may have kept General Abraxas' wrath at bay this time but I don't know what will happen if you fail again."

Sammy huffed. "My day was fine, Father, thank you for asking. And *I'm* fine too. I appreciate your obvious concern."

"We don't have time for your childish tantrums!" he yelled as he stood before her. The chair, upended by his sudden movement, slid across the stone floor. "It's time for you to grow up and assume your place as a Fire Warrior!"

"I am acting like a Fire Warrior. But right now, I'm also trying to have a conversation with my father."

"Right now, I need competent warriors far more than I need a daughter," he replied harshly.

"Why are you acting like this?" Sammy cried, the tears spilling past her cheeks. "You never used to be like this. It's like I got my powers early and now you want nothing to do with me."

Lord Balor turned away from his daughter and pinched the bridge of his nose, as though warding away a budding headache.

"Sammy," he said, his tone quite a bit softened from the start of their conversation, "there are things going on that you don't understand."

"Then explain them to me."

Her father sighed. "I can't."

Sammy stood and walked to the window. She gestured outside, toward the cavern beyond. "Then go explain it to the other High Lords. The other clans of the Fire Warriors are as confused as I am about what you're trying to do. Why are you suddenly so interested in killing the Wind Caste? We've spent all this time waiting our turn. Now, all of this sudden, they can't die quickly enough for you."

"I don't care what the other clans think," Balor

replied angrily. "Our clan has been chosen to lead the way for the rest of the Fire Caste. You should be proud!"

"Chosen by whom?" Sammy asked, perplexed.

"By powers that you couldn't possibly begin to understand!" he said angrily, turning sharply toward her.

Sammy's expression softened and confusion crept into her eyes. "What powers? What could possibly hold power over one of the Fire Lords?"

Lord Balor waved his hand dismissively. "We're done here. You'll leave tomorrow with General Abraxas. Don't fail us again."

He walked to the door but paused in the entryway. Slowly, he looked over his shoulder to where his daughter still stood by the windowsill.

"Is there anything else you need before you leave?" he asked with genuine compassion.

When Sammy didn't respond, Lord Balor walked out of the room and closed the door softly behind him.

After he retreated, Sammy turned back toward the room.

"Yeah, there is something," she said softly. "I need my father back. And I think I know where to go to find out where he went."

The castle was silent as she crept down the hall leading to the throne room. The heavy oil on the buckles of her leather armor kept them from creaking as she moved, leaving her silent as she slid down the hallway. Despite the faint glow from the lava outside, most of the castle was asleep, adhering to an obscure sense of day and night within the perpetually lit cave.

She peered around the corner of the hall and toward the large, throne room doors. For a brief moment, she held to the hope that the doors to the throne room would be unguarded. Sadly, a pair of guards stood stoically to either side of them, their gazed affixed firmly ahead.

Sighing, she stepped around the corner and approached the men. The guard closest to her shifted his gaze but he relaxed visibly as he recognized her.

"Lady Balor," the guard said as she approached. "What brings you here at this late hour?"

"Lord Balor wishes me to retrieve something left behind in the throne room," she replied, hoping her nervousness wasn't evident in her voice.

The second guard cleared his throat. "I'm sorry, my Lady, but we have strict orders not to let anyone into the throne room without either Lord Balor's or General Abraxas' direct authorization."

Sammy felt herself sweating beneath the form-fitting armor, though she realized it had little to do with the heat. This would be her only chance to explore before she left again in the morning. If she couldn't convince the guards to let her pass, then she would never have another opportunity like this one.

She thought about how her father might react in a similar situation. He had an uncanny ability to convince Fire Warriors to do his bidding through a combination of confidence and unspoken threats.

"I told you," she said, assuming a more regal tone, "that I'm coming on my father's behalf."

The nearest guard swallowed hard and Sammy

immediately knew that her presence was affecting their resolve.

"I—I can't let you in," he stammered. "Not without Lord Balor explicitly telling me to do so."

Sammy frowned, a move that was as much a calculated expression as one of general disappointment. She knew her options were fading quickly away, which left her only with one final gambit.

"Fine," she said angrily. "Then let's go wake up my father. Let's go wake up Lord Balor and tell him that you've refused to follow his direct orders and denied his only child entrance into his throne room at his behest. Which of you is brave enough to be the one to tell him? You? Or maybe you?"

The two guards looked at one another nervously. Sammy knew she was following a dangerous path. If either guard called her bluff, then she didn't even want to fathom the reaction and punishment she might receive from her father.

After what seemed like an eternity, the closest guard turned back to her.

"My apologies, Lady Balor. Please go right ahead."

They opened the doors for her and she stepped into the vaulted throne room. As the doors clicked loudly into place behind her, she released the breath that she didn't even realize she'd been holding. Her heart raced in her chest and she was forced to lean against a pillar for support as her legs threatened to give out beneath her.

Steadying herself, Sammy hurried across the throne room until she reached the raised dais. She slid past the ornate stone throne and pushed aside the hanging tapestry behind it.

She immediately felt crestfallen. She had assumed that after watching her father disappear into the secret passage, the trigger to open the door would be obvious. To her dismay, it wasn't. She stared at the towering gray cobblestone wall, knowing that one of these stones was the one that needed to be pressed to open the secret passage.

Sammy leaned in close to the stonework and examined the varyingly sized stones. Some were nearly the size of her head, while others were carved to fill in gaps, leaving them slightly smaller than her fist. There were literally hundreds of possibilities standing before her and her time was far too short to search them all.

Nervously, she pressed against some of stones around her head level. From where she had spied through the crack in the door, she had seen her father pressing a stone higher on the wall. Her efforts offered nothing in return.

She wanted to bang her fists against the rocks in frustration but didn't for fear of alerting the guards. Sammy chewed on her bottom lip and tugged absently on the end of her long braid as she stared at the wall.

"Come on, Sammy," she whispered. "Think! This is a secret passage behind the throne of one of the Fire Lords. Maybe…"

She paused as she looked at the wall again.

"Maybe the trigger stone gives off heat?" she said, without much hope of success.

She closed her eyes and held her open palm out

before her. Slowly, she ran it past the stones, concentrating on detecting any heat emanating from the stonework.

As her hand passed a stone just above her right shoulder, she felt a violent tug in her gut, as though the cobblestones were pulling at her very soul. The tug grew stronger and she felt her power flowing unbidden through her hand.

She tried to pull her hand away but it seemed transfixed over the now glowing stone. It shone with an inner light, like magma was boiling right underneath its surface. Sammy felt drained and she tried in vain again to pull her hand back.

The heat in her hand grew more intense, to the point that it was causing her physical pain. Flames poured soundlessly from her hand and were as quickly absorbed into the cobblestone wall. Sammy coughed, as the stone seemed to drain even the air from her lungs.

When she thought she couldn't take any more and unconsciousness threatened at the corners of her vision, the flow of power suddenly stopped. The burning stone flared a quick, vibrant red before returning to its lackluster gray.

The wall before her shifted and grated across the floor as the secret passage revealed itself. Sammy groaned and was forced to sit on the steps of the dais to regain her composure before daring to enter the tunnel.

Whatever was down this tunnel, she had to remind herself, it had drastically changed her father. It had stripped away the compassionate man that had existed before her powers manifested when she turned eighteen. Whatever was down this tunnel, she swore it had caused Lord Balor to show fear when she asked him about it in her room. Anything that caused her father to fear wasn't to be taken lightly.

When she felt confident that she could walk without stumbling on weak legs, Sammy stood and entered the narrow tunnel.

The heat within the tunnel was oppressive, far more than she was even used to within the lava-filled cavern behind her. Her nervous sweat evaporated as soon as it left her skin, leaving her feeling parched and lightheaded. It only grew hotter and more stifling as she walked down the gently sloping tunnel.

The way ahead was completely dark and she was forced to create a small flame in her hand to illuminate the passage. The tunnel was made of worked stone and she passed massive rock support pillars every few feet, causing her to turn sideways to fit between them.

She followed the tunnel for a long ways, constantly wandering deeper and deeper into the earth. The heat grew more intense until her skin seemed to crawl. Sammy found herself absently scratching the exposed skin around her forearms and neck as it itched more and more in the heat. Her breathing became labored and she felt lightheaded, as though the oxygen were being burned out of the air around her.

Heaving, Sammy paused and leaned against one of the support pillars. She leaned her head against the stone, hoping the coolness would alleviate some of her discomfort but even it radiated heat.

She glanced over her shoulder, wondering if it was worth discovering what at the end of this tunnel had so greatly affected her father. Coughing loudly in the narrow stone passage, she wondered if it would be worth discovering it if she lacked the energy to make it back to the castle alive.

The difference between the loving father from her youth and the callous man who now sat on the throne drove her forward again. Sammy pushed away from the pillar and staggered back down the descending hallway.

She wondered how long she had been walking. Ten minutes? Thirty? An hour? The guards surely had noticed she wasn't coming back by now. She wondered who they would tell; if her father or General Abraxas would be the first person they awoke to warn about her betrayal. Even if she made it back to the surface, she might face a short-lived victory before facing either or both of their wraths.

As she wandered down the hall, she wondered why she was putting herself through this. She was betraying everything she'd known, everything she'd been taught since birth. Despite her concerns, she knew why she was searching for answers. Xander. Just the thought of his name sent relieving chills all over her body. It made no sense that she'd long for him after only a few days together but being apart from him was leaving her in anguish. Whatever was pulling them together, it was far more supernatural than a normal attraction.

While her thoughts were consumed with memories of Xander, she reached the end of the narrow hall. The passage gave way to a cavernous room. The walls of the room stretched to either side of her, disappearing in shadows far beyond reach of the meager flame in her hand. Glancing upward, she could barely tell the curve of the ceiling before it, too, vanished into gloomy darkness.

Nervously, she caused the flame in her hand to grow until the tips of the flames licked high above her head. Even with the intense flame burning in her hand, the massive room swallowed her light with its darkness well before it lit to either the ceiling or any other nearby walls.

The light slowly faded back to flickering candlelight in her hand before she extinguished it completely, casting the entire room into blinding darkness.

It wasn't the intimidation she felt at the dauntingly enormous room that caused her to extinguish her flame. Instead, it was a feeling in her gut—an inordinate sense that she wasn't alone in the room. In such a dark chamber, her flame was a beacon for the creature that resided within.

Sammy reached out and gently touched the wall behind her. She slid her feet on the stone floor to make sure she didn't trip as she backed against it. Each scrape of her booted foot sounded like steel grating against steel to her heightened hearing. Her own heartbeat sounded like a drum pounding as it rushed past her ears. She could feel her eyes dilating as they tried to adjust to the inky blackness but she couldn't see anything this far underground.

"I hear you breathing, fleshling."

The voice sounded like a whisper but was full

enough to fill the cavernous room. It sent shivers of fear washing over her.

"*Come closer*," the unseen voice hissed. "*I can already taste your fear in the air. It's intoxicating.*"

"Who's there?" Sammy said, her body shaking uncontrollably. "Show yourself!"

A jet of flame roared across the far end of the room. Its sudden brilliance was blinding after the complete darkness in which she'd been standing. Sammy raised a hand to block away the sudden light but it faded as quickly as it had come, leaving her once again in the all-consuming black.

Sammy's heart pounded and she slid along the wall toward the passage, eager to be gone from this living nightmare. Her foot nudged against a loose rock on the ground and it tumbled away, bouncing loudly against the protruding stonework.

Across the room, a single, massive orb of an eye opened and stared at the frozen Fire Warrior. The reptilian eye glowed a sickly yellow; its vertical pupil contracting as it stared across the cavern. The draconic orb blinked once, disappearing momentarily before reappearing and staring at Sammy.

"*Leaving so soon, fleshling? I'll see you again.*"

Ignoring her previous concerns about her light, Sammy ignited a flame in her hand and ran into the narrow passage. Mocking laughter followed her as she fled quickly.

The trip back up the inclined hall was far quicker than she remembered on her descent. The secret doorway was still opened and she handily knocked aside the dangling tapestry before staggering back into the throne room.

She sobbed loudly and collapsed onto the dais' staircase. Burying her face in her arms, she let the tears flow until she was certain she could risk standing again.

Sammy dusted herself off and hastily wiped at her eyes. Clearing her throat, she walked as confidently as possible toward the throne room doors. No one had met her when she emerged from the secret passage but she knew it was only a matter of time before she had to confront the elder Fire Warriors.

She pushed on the throne room doors and exited. The two guards were still at their post and nodded politely to her as she walked past them. Neither tried to stop her, nor did anyone else emerge to confront her.

Sammy maintained her composure until she reached her room. When the door clicked closed behind her, Sammy's knees went weak and she slid down to the floor.

Something was definitely controlling her father, she realized with horror. Only it was far more terrifying than she would have ever believed. Whatever it was, she and the Wind Warriors now had one more horrifying thing to worry about.

CHAPTER 13

Xander parried Thea's downward swing. She quickly stepped back, far quicker than Xander would have believe possible from an older woman, and dropped into a sweeping kick. He leapt into the air and caught an updraft that launched him over her head. He landed gracefully behind her and spun in a swing that should have connected his wooden training sword with the side of her head.

Instead, his sword cut through empty space as Thea dropped into a crouch. She drove her own training sword forward and jabbed him in the gut with the blunted tip.

Xander exhaled loudly and doubled over. His sword tumbled from his limp hand and clattered onto the tiled floor seconds before he joined it.

"Are you okay?" Thea asked, though Xander doubted she really much cared.

He held up a finger and begged her to wait a moment as he regained his breath. When he could finally catch a breath through his deflated diaphragm, he pushed himself up onto his knees and blinked away the tears in his eyes.

"Are you okay?" she repeated.

"Yeah, great," he groaned.

He stood against his body's protests. His legs felt like jelly, not just from the sparring he'd been doing with Thea but also from the flight lessons with Giovanni, the wind sculpting with Alicia, and the defensive techniques with Patrick. His training was nonstop, leaving little time for rest. Most opportunities to sleep were stolen from him with thoughts of Sammy, Sean, and his family.

"What's the point of learning to swing a sword?" he asked as he rubbed the spreading bruise on his stomach. "We're Wind Warriors. Shouldn't I be learning another skill involving wind?"

"This is a lesson that involves your power. The biggest difficulty when learning to swordfight is being able to keep a clear mind and think through your parries and counterattacks. What you're learning with the others is important but it won't keep you calm in a fight. If you can't keep your thoughts straight when fighting for your life then it won't matter how many wind skills you've mastered."

Xander sighed but she shook her head unapologetically.

"Again," she demanded.

He snuck away in between his lessons and slipped into the middle dome of the island. The dimly lit interior was cool compared to the sunbaked exterior. The marble outside reflected the bright sunlight, which left the exterior of the buildings hot but left the interiors comfortably cool.

Xander paused in the entryway and let his eyes adjust to the dim light. As the room came into focus, he could see his grandfather moving around a seated figure. The man in the middle of the room had a beard that reached past his knees as he sat. His hair was long and unkempt, though his grandfather affectionately brushed out some of the knots that had formed. Gray streaked the man's hair and his skin was wrinkled and peppered with liver spots.

He hadn't realized anyone in the clan was older than his grandfather until he met Robert. As far as Xander could tell, he never left the chair and probably hadn't seen the sun in years. It was his power alone that kept the island afloat and the waterspout concealing their location.

The energy in the air was palpable. He could practically taste the electric charge as he moved toward the two elder men.

His grandfather looked up as he came close and the old man flashed a smile to his grandson.

"How is your training going?"

Xander shook his head and laughed to himself. The simple chuckle hurt his body. "It's going well. Brutal, but good."

His grandfather looked down as he pulled the brush through Robert's hair once again. "You look worried."

"I guess I am," Xander said. He walked over to one of the crates nearby and sat down with a grimace. "I'm worried about my mom and dad. I just wish I knew they were okay."

His grandfather nodded. "Bart's been watching them closely. If they were in trouble, he'd let us know right away."

Xander didn't seem relieved.

"Would you like me to bring Bart back and let you know they're still safe?"

"No," Xander admitted. "I'm glad we have someone taking care of them. It's just... well, a month ago I was a normal, unmotivated college student. I couldn't even decide what to do with my life. Now I'm thrust into the middle of an ages-old war between elemental powers. It's just a little daunting."

"I wish I could say it's going to get easier."

He nodded. Looking over, he gestured toward the seated warrior. "Can he hear us?"

His grandfather looked down as he pulled the brush through Robert's long hair. "Of course. He's deep in concentration but he still knows what's going on around him."

"What if he stopped concentrating?"

His grandfather arched an eyebrow. "I guess the island would crash into the sea and everyone who couldn't fly would be killed."

Xander swallowed hard.

"It's a good thing everyone on the island can fly, huh?" his grandfather joked.

Xander stood and walked back toward the door, squinting as he emerged into the light. He looked back over his shoulder into the cool depths of the room.

"I'm glad you're here with me, Grandpa."

"I'm glad I'm here with you too."

Smiling, he turned back toward his next Wind Warrior trainer.

CHAPTER 14

Sammy and General Abraxas emerged from the chasm in the rock face and looked out on the barren landscape. The glaring desert sun beat down on them but neither Fire Warrior minded the intense heat.

Abraxas raised a hand to block the sunlight as he scanned the horizon. The California desert was empty as far as he could see.

"This is what they're willing to die to defend?" the General grumbled. "It doesn't look like much."

Sammy looked toward the General. His clean-shaven head was marred by a series of clan tattoos. His beady dark eyes looked down the length of a hawk-like nose. The point of his nose was mirrored in the downturned points of his mouth, perpetually frozen in a disapproving frown.

"This is the desert," Sammy tried to explain. "The residential areas look quite a bit different."

General Abraxas huffed in displeasure. "Let's complete our mission and be done with this place. The next time I look on the surface, it should be at the head of a conquering army."

Sammy nodded but didn't reply. Her mind spun

with her memories of the horrifying eye deep in the cavern. She tried to rationalize what she had seen, that it had been part of her paranoia as she searched the hidden passage, but she couldn't get the memory of that roaring voice out of her mind.

"Find us a mode of transportation," Abraxas demanded.

"Excuse me?" Sammy said as she tried to brush aside the disturbing memory.

"I told you to find us a mode of transportation."

Sammy looked around the empty desert and sighed. It would be a long walk before she could find a car but at least it would give her a chance to think in peace. Aside from the monster in the cavern, she still had a maddening swirl of thoughts about Xander bouncing around in her mind. She almost welcomed the chance to be left with her thoughts, far away from General Abraxas.

With a sigh, she began jogging out into the empty desert.

When she was far out of sight, Abraxas motioned back into the cavern and a squad of masked Fire Warriors emerged.

"You know your mission," he said to the lead warrior. "Find the rest of the Wind Warriors and kill them all."

The Fire Warriors nodded in unison before turning the opposite direction Sammy ran and disappearing quickly into the expansive desert.

A few hours later, the pair was driving down Interstate 40 on their way out of California. Sammy sat behind the wheel and let the wind from the open window whip through her long blonde braid that hung over her shoulder. She set her arm on the windowsill and let her hand catch the wind as it blew past the car. The metal on the windowsill was incredibly hot and she heard the sizzle on her skin but she didn't remove her arm. Fire Warriors were incredibly resistant to the heat but they were far from immune to the flames that they wielded. She just taught her mind to ignore the pain until it became unbearable.

"This was the best vehicle you could get?" Abraxas asked. He frowned as he looked around the interior of the 1985 Buick.

"Beggars can't be choosers."

"And you killed the owner so we couldn't be traced?"

Sammy's frown matched that of Abraxas. She could have told him the truth—that she had merely stolen the car when it was left unattended—but he wouldn't have approved of leaving potential witnesses.

"Where are we going?" she asked, avoiding his question altogether.

"Don't concern yourself with that."

"I am concerned and you should be too. Unless you suddenly learned how to drive in that cave of yours, I'm going to be driving us the whole way. I'd like to know where we're going."

General Abraxas turned toward her and smiled. His pointed teeth made his smile look more like a predatory sneer.

"East," he said finally.

Sammy sighed and turned her attention back to

the road. In the distance, between the wavering heat lines coming off the road, she could see a few small structures and some cars parked along the interstate. Abraxas noticed them immediately after she did and he turned sharply toward her.

"What is this? Did you betray me?"

"It's nothing," Sammy replied. "Just a highway patrol checkpoint. They're normal when you leave California."

"If you or they try anything," he said, leaving the threat hanging in the air.

"That won't be necessary. Just let me do the talking."

She slowed the car to a decelerating coast as they approached the checkpoint. California Highway Patrol officers stood beside the road, asking questions of the drivers as they passed out of the state.

When waved forward, Sammy drove up beside the officer.

"Good morning, ma'am, sir. We just need to ask you a couple questions before you go on your way."

"No problem, Officer," Sammy said with a confident smile.

"Are you transporting any fruit?"

"No."

"Are you transporting any live animals?"

"Nope."

The officer tilted his hat back as he looked at the low-cut half-shirt that Sammy was wearing. "Where are you heading?"

Sammy smiled but her gut twisted. "East."

She was relieved when the officer smiled, thinking her answer was a joke.

"Really, now? What are you and your father heading East for?"

General Abraxas leaned across the seat and smiled his sharpened teeth at the officer. "The end of times, Officer."

CHAPTER 15

Sean pulled back the curtain and glanced outside the window for the hundredth time that day. Nothing obscured his view of the parking lot and the road beyond. Despite the densely parked cars in the lot, he saw no sign of the blonde-haired fire wielders who had attacked him and Jessica. The strangers seemed to have gone as they came.

He let go of the curtain and let it fall back into place. Though it seemed as though the Fire Warriors hadn't followed him to his apartment, Sean refused to let go of the nervous breath he was holding.

After all the time that had passed since the fire in the park near Xander's house, no one had heard from his best friend. On the few rare occasions in which Sean ventured out from his apartment, he had asked some of Xander's former classmates if they had seen him, which none had. He hadn't been to the school nor returned to his parent's home. His friend had, for all intents and purposed, vanished.

Pushing himself off the couch, Sean walked toward the kitchen. His refrigerator was running dangerously low on food but there was always enough to make into a decent snack. He knew the jokes Xander would make about eating as a nervous habit but Sean felt justified in being nervous.

As he opened the refrigerator and started pulling out lunchmeat, he heard a gentle knock on the door. He froze, his hand unmoving around the plastic turkey container.

"Go away," he whispered into the room.

He didn't know who was at the door but he honestly didn't care. He doubted Xander would knock so gingerly and no one else would be bringing him good news.

Sean slid the turkey package out of the refrigerator as quietly as possible and softly closed the door. Logically, he knew that the person on the other side of the door couldn't hear his refrigerator closing. Normal people couldn't hear that, he had to remind himself. His best friend could control the wind. The people that were hunting him could throw fire from their hands. There was no telling if super hearing was another of their hidden super powers.

As he reached toward the stack of bread, the same person knocked again at the door. Glancing around nervously, his eyes fell on the bottle opener magnet hanging from the fridge. Sean pulled it off the fridge and held it in front of him defensively. He left the kitchen and walked toward the door.

When the person knocked for the third time, it seemed far more insistent.

"Who's there?" Sean asked, trying to force some mock confidence into his voice.

"It's Jessica."

Sean visibly sagged with disappointment. He

almost wished it were one of the Fire Warriors.

"What do you want?"

"Can you open the door?" she said pleadingly. "Please?"

Sean sighed as he reached out and unlocked the door. As he pulled the door open, he was surprised to see a fairly disheveled Jessica standing before him. Loose tendrils from her shoddy ponytail hung over her face. She didn't seem to be wearing any makeup, aside from the obvious lip gloss that caused the unnatural shine on her lips. She wore a loose-fitting blouse that was heavily wrinkled. Sean couldn't remember ever seeing her looking anything less than fully composed. Despite her obviously harried expression, she still found the reserve to frown at her nemesis.

"Sean," she said.

"Wicked Witch of the West."

She opened her mouth to offer a sharp retort but quickly thought better of it.

"What are you doing here?" he asked.

"I didn't know where else to go," she admitted sheepishly.

"You don't have GPS on your broom?"

Jessica smiled humorlessly. "Are you done?"

"Not by a long shot," he replied.

"Go ahead. Get them all out of your system."

"You figured the inside of my apartment would keep you out of the life-ending rain? Your flying monkeys ran out of likely candidates to kidnap? You do realize I don't even have a dog named Toto, right?"

"Can I please come in now?" Something in her

voice caught Sean off guard and the humor seemed to bleed out of the situation. He nodded and stepped out of the way.

As she entered the apartment, he closed and locked the door behind her.

She walked a few steps inside before turning toward him. Glancing down, she noticed the bottle opener in his hand.

"What's that for?"

Sean looked down and seemed equally surprised to see it still clutched in his hand. "I don't know. I figured I could stab someone with it if I had to."

"You got that from the kitchen?" she asked. "Why didn't you just get a knife?"

Sean was genuinely dumbfounded by the question, especially since he didn't have a logical answer. He tossed the bottle opener onto the couch angrily.

"Shut up. You still haven't even told me why you're here."

"I told you, I didn't know where else to go. I've been totally freaked out ever since the other night. I've barely slept. I've barely eaten." Her voice lowered to a soft whisper. "I think one of those blonde guys has been following me."

"And you came here?" Sean yelled before throwing a hand over his mouth to silence himself.

"You came here?" he said again in a harsh whisper.

"I told you. I didn't know where else to go. No one else would believe me if I told them some guy set my car on fire using only his hands. You have no idea how hard it was to explain what happened to my car to my dad. I had to give him some totally crazy story about a drunk homeless guy."

Sean stormed past her before pausing in the doorway to the kitchen. "Did you even stop to consider what would happen if you really were being followed? You could have led them right to me!"

"Oh, yeah Sean. You're practically 007. Everyone's trying to hunt…"

The words faded from her lips as someone knocked on the door. The stern knock was the complete antithesis to Jessica's soft knocking from earlier.

Jessica started to whimper but Sean stepped forward and clamped his hand down over her mouth.

"Stay quiet," he whispered.

Sean slipped past her and eased his way to the door. Leaning forward, he glanced out the peephole. The man on the other side of the door was unmistakable. His close-cropped blonde hair and dark leather tunic looked identical to the man that tried to kill Sean at Xander's house.

"Is it?" Jessica asked, leaving the end of question hanging.

Sean nodded as he inched his way back to her. The Fire Warrior banged loudly again on the door.

"Let's just not answer," she offered. "He'll go away eventually, right?"

"He followed you here, remember? If he wants in, he'll just burn the door down."

"Then what to do we do?"

Sean stroked his hairless chin. "You're going to open the door."

"Oh no, I'm not!" she replied sternly. Jessica placed her hands on her hips and flipped the few hanging tendrils of her blonde hair out of her face. "If you want the door open, you'll have to be a big boy and do it yourself."

Sean frowned. "You're going to open the door so that I can attack him. Unless you want to attack him, that is."

Jessica quickly shook her head. "No, that's fine. I'll get the door."

Sean disappeared into the kitchen as Jessica moved to the door.

"Ready?" she asked.

Sean leaned around the corner and nodded. She held up three fingers and silently counted down. When she dropped the last finger, she unlocked the door and threw it open.

The Fire Warrior on the other side seemed temporarily startled. He quickly overcame his surprise and stepped into the room, chasing after the retreating Jessica.

She stumbled backward and fell into the middle of the room. The tears already threatened to fall down her face as she stared at the frightening warrior entering the room.

The Fire Warrior smiled wickedly and extended his hand. The tips of his fingers ignited as flames danced over his hand.

"Sean?" Jessica sobbed.

"Here I am," he replied, stepping through the kitchen door. He held up the large red cylinder in his hands and pointed the nozzle at the confused Fire

Warrior.

"Suck on this, dude."

Sean squeezed the handle to the fire extinguisher and the far end of the room was consumed in white powder. The cloud sprayed over the Fire Warrior, extinguishing the flames on his hand, as he was covered from head to toe in white foam. Sean held down the handle until the small extinguisher ran dry and sputtered in his hand. As the cloud settled, the entire room was coated in white foam, to include an undignified Jessica who sat sputtering on the floor.

The Fire Warrior coughed loudly as he seemed frozen in confusion. Sean paused, realizing that he hadn't thought through his plan beyond spraying the man with the extinguisher. Despite him being coated in inflammable foam, Sean was still facing a vastly physically superior man.

"I really didn't think this through," he muttered as the Fire Warrior reclaimed his wits and stormed toward Sean.

Sean gulped and dropped the extinguisher, as though releasing the weapon would alleviate him of the blame.

The warrior reached Sean in a few large strides and grabbed him by his shirt. Despite Sean's weight, the Fire Warrior lifted him from his feet and pinned him against the wall.

"Can't we talk about this?" Sean said meekly.

The blonde warrior merely growled at him. The Fire Warrior leaned in, his nose mere inches away from Sean's face. Sean could practically see the fire burning behind his dark eyes.

A hollow thud suddenly echoed through the room. The smoldering glare in the warrior's eyes disappeared as his eyes rolled up into his head. The Fire Warrior pitched to the side, his arms going limp and releasing Sean in the process.

Jessica stood behind the warrior, clinging to the extinguisher like a club. She looked nervously at the unconscious Fire Warrior.

"You think he's going to be okay?" she asked.

"Who cares?" Sean replied, laughing nervously.

Jessica dropped the extinguisher and smiled weakly. Sean returned the smile before spreading his arms and motioning her forward.

"You did great," he said as they hugged one another in relief.

For a long moment, they stood straddling the unconscious blonde man, embraced in each other's arms. Suddenly, as though remembering her surroundings, Jessica stiffened.

"You know that we're only hugging because I'm so relieved to still be alive, right? Nothing more?"

Sean nodded quickly. "Of course. Sure."

"I mean," she continued, "if it weren't for the fact that someone just tried to kill us, we wouldn't even be caught dead in the same room, right?"

"Sure," he said softly as he took in the smell of her hair cascading past his face.

She paused and turned her face toward him. "Did you just smell my hair?"

Sean arched an eyebrow as his face flushed

in embarrassment. "No, no, of course not," he laughed nervously. "That would have been weird!"

"This moment's over," she said sternly, pushing him back.

As they separated, Sean inadvertently kicked the unconscious Fire Warrior. The man groaned softly. The pair looked at each other again, suddenly remembering what brought them together in the first place.

"What are we going to do about him?" she asked.

Sean shrugged. "I guess we tie him up?"

"He makes fire out of the air, Sean. What's to stop him from just burning through his ropes?"

"Then we put him in the shower?" he offered. Her withering stare ended that train of thought. "No, you're right. That was a stupid idea."

Jessica shrugged. "Yeah, but I don't really have a better one."

They returned to the living room, both exhausted from the exertion of moving the large Fire Warrior. In the background, they could both hear the faint sound of running water.

They both collapsed on the couch. Sean leaned his head back and closed his eyes, wishing he could just go to sleep. There was always the chance that when he woke up, this would have all just been a miserable nightmare.

Sean rubbed his eyes before stealing a glance at Jessica. Despite her wrinkled clothing and the layer of extinguisher foam that clung infuriatingly to her body, she still looked amazing. She was every bit the sorority girl he had found so attractive and equally despised.

"So what do we do now?" he asked.

"You could start by telling me what this is all about."

Sean sat upright. "What makes you think I have any idea what's going on here?"

Jessica narrowed her eyes. "Because they were chasing you when they set fire to my car. This is all your fault."

"Time out!" he replied angrily. "The only reason they were after me was because I went to talk to Xander's parents. This all started because he discovered he…"

Sean quickly shut his mouth after realizing he was sharing far more than he should.

"He discovered what?" she said threateningly.

"Oh, nothing."

"Oh no, you don't. Spill."

Sean glanced over his shoulder, almost hoping the Fire Warrior would emerge from the bathroom. When the blonde man didn't appear, Sean scowled in his direction.

"Let's hear it, Sean," she said.

Sean sighed and turned back to her. "All right, but you can't tell anyone what I'm about to tell you."

"Sure, whatever."

He took a deep breath. "You may want to sit down for this."

She looked around at the couch on which she was currently sitting on. "I *am* sitting down."

"No, I mean like *sit down* sit down."

"You're an idiot. And you're stalling."

"Fine," Sean replied. "These guys are after Xander because… because he's a superhero. There, I said it."

Jessica stared at him unblinking. The pencil thin line of her lips didn't turn up or down but remained emotionlessly bloodless as she pressed them together.

"I'm sticking to my previous statement. You're an idiot."

She started to stand but Sean was quicker. He jumped to his feet and moved in front of her.

"Oh, sure. You have no trouble believing that a bunch of psychotic pyromaniacs are trying to kill us but the fact that your ex-boyfriend is a superhero is just much too far-fetched."

"I know Xander. He's no superhero."

"He was also completely devoted to you up until some new blonde wandered by. Did you know him well enough to know that was going to happen?"

Jessica frowned but her eyes quickly watered. She angrily reached up and wiped them away rather than let him see her cry.

"Listen, Jessica," he said, suddenly feeling guilty. He extended his hand. "That was cheap of me. Can we call a truce for a little while, at least until we figure out what's going on?"

She glanced at the hand before reaching up and shaking. "We still need to figure out what we're going to do next. We can't really leave a guy in the shower forever."

Sean turned and walked over to the desk on the other side of the living room. His laptop was sitting closed on the desktop and he flipped it open. The soft white glow of the screen washed over him as he took a seat. Jessica stood from the couch and walked over.

"What are you doing?"

Sean opened a new browser window and began typing. "There's got to be something on these fire guys somewhere on the internet. People with super powers don't just suddenly appear without someone noticing."

She leaned over his shoulder, genuinely impressed. "You really think 'guys who can use fire' is really going to turn up a decent search?"

"Well, what would you recommend?"

Jessica shrugged before gently pushing his hands off the keyboard. She typed "strange fire phenomenon" into the search window and hit enter. The browser filled with results on spontaneous human combustion and fire rainbows. Jessica pointed to the bottom of the search window where there was an article about unexplained fires erupting throughout an Italian town.

"That one," she said.

Sean clicked on it. As the window loaded, Jessica began reading intently. Sean stole a glance at her out of the corner of his eye. He hated himself for thinking it, but even without makeup Jessica was still incredibly attractive. He couldn't believe she was actually in his apartment.

"If you keep looking at me like that, I'm going to poke you in the eyes."

Sean flushed. "Look at you like what?" he replied indignantly.

Jessica looked away from the screen and flashed a condescending smile. "Like I'm a hamburger."

"Really? A fat joke? Real mature, Jessica."

Jessica's gaze turned back to the computer screen. "I call them like I see them."

Just like that, his attraction to her faded and he was reminded why he disliked her so much.

Before he could reply again, she reached past him and started typing. "Check this out."

The screen became a map of the Earth with large sections marked with a series of overlapping red dots.

"I just did a search for strange fire-related natural events and this is what I got. These are tons of forest fires in California. There are the fires in Naples, Italy. There are currently three volcanoes erupting around the world."

"Isn't that what volcanoes do?"

Jessica shot him a warning glare. "Yes, but these have been dormant for a long time and are suddenly waking up at the same time."

"So what? We can't stop a volcano. We were lucky to beat up a single one of those fire guys. We don't exactly have a big enough shower to hang over a volcano."

"We really only have one choice," Jessica replied, pushing away from the computer. "We need to find Xander."

CHAPTER 16

The Buick rumbled down the narrow street. It pulled dangerously to the right and the wheels connected with the rumble strip. A loud buzz sounded for a second before Sammy pulled the car back into her lane.

"Are you okay?" Abraxas asked, though she doubted he asked for anything more than concern for his own well-being.

"I'm fine," she said. Her words were choked with emotion as she drove down the familiar streets.

"Good."

She swallowed hard, trying to force down the ball of fear that was lodged firmly in her throat. "Why are we here?"

Abraxas grinned wickedly. "We're hunting a rodent. It's not always possible to chase a rodent, especially when they decide to hide from you. Therefore, if they won't come to you, you bait them. Give them something worth chasing and then crush them when they're in the open."

Sammy looked up as they drove past the city limits sign. She saw the large painted sun and the broad white letters that read, *Welcome to White Halls.*

"If you're out there, Xander," she whispered quietly enough not to be overheard, "please come home. I can't do this alone."

She pulled the Buick over and parked against the curb. A few other cars passed the Fire Warriors as they sat in the car in silence.

A group of college students walked past on the sidewalk, laughing and teasing one another as they strolled toward the restaurant a few blocks away. In the front of the group, a guy and girl walked with their arms linked and broad smiles plastered across their faces. The sight caused a pang in Sammy's chest. It hadn't been that long ago in this town that she and Xander had walked into the spring formal, linked arm in arm like the college kids she now watched.

From the corner of her eye, she stole a glance to General Abraxas. The remorseful longing that she felt was nowhere to be seen on his face. He instead scowled at the kids, as though their happiness was a personal affront.

"What are we doing here?" she asked again.

He ignored her question and continued staring out the window. Reaching over, he rolled down his window and let the cool breeze wash over him. His nostrils flared as he took in the odor of the small town. After a brief smell, his brow furrowed in disgust and he spat out the window.

"This place stinks," he said.

"It's called fresh air."

The General shook his head. "It's not fresh. I can smell it, haunting just below the surface. It's there, hanging like a poison cloud just below the breeze. It's the toxin of humanity. It's the smell of strip-mined mountains. It's the smell of polluted rivers. It's the smell of noxious clouds of smoke billowing out of their factories. It's permeated everything they touch."

Sammy huffed. "You're just spouting the same rhetoric I've heard from my father since I was born. I've seen the surface world. It's not nearly as bad as you seem to believe."

"It doesn't matter what you believe," he said, smiling wickedly. "The Wind Caste will fall and we will ravage the world of man. Burn it back to the Earth. Nothing will stop us."

"He'll try," the words slipped out before she could stop them. Sammy immediately flushed with embarrassment.

Rather than seeming upset, General Abraxas' smile widened. "You mean the Wind Warrior. He'll try. And he'll die, just like all the rest of their kind. And when the last of them die by my hand, then the rest of the world will share their fate."

Angrily, Sammy opened her door and climbed out of the car. She slammed it behind her and stormed across the street. As she walked, she heard the soft click of his door being opened as well.

She didn't know what to do. Abraxas was right—the Wind Caste didn't stand a chance against the Fire Warriors. Their power was created to feed the flames, meaning that it would take an exceptional amount of power to defeat a trained group of warriors. The fact that they defeated her warriors previously only proved that her warriors were inexperienced and overly confident—it hardly proved that the Wind Warriors were truly that powerful.

The General crossed the road and walked up behind her. "You can't stop the inevitable."

She kept her back to him, choosing instead to watch him through the reflection in the glass storefront. She watched him turn away from her and sniff the air once again. He smiled as he caught the scent of what he was looking for. Suddenly, she felt it as well. She felt the small twinge in her stomach, like something crawling across her skin. She had felt that sensation once before, when Xander first used his powers. Someone was using elemental powers nearby.

"There's a Wind Warrior in town," he whispered.

Sammy paled. She couldn't imagine Xander would be foolish enough to come back home so soon after she tried to kill him but the General wasn't wrong. Someone in the town had used elemental powers. It wasn't one of the Fire Warriors; the power used had a different sensation, one to which she wasn't accustomed. It had to be a Wind Warrior.

"Tell me, Lady Balor," the General said as he smiled and showed his rows of sharpened teeth. "Where did your young Wind Warrior live?"

Sammy shook her head as beads of sweat broke out across her forehead. She suddenly knew what the General had in mind.

"I don't know," she lied. Though she had never

been to his house, she had seen his house after following him home after school.

General Abraxas' smile disappeared and he glowered at Sammy. "Don't lie to me, girl!"

He reached out and clenched her arm, his fingers searing against her skin. She screamed out in pain and her knees buckled as his grip tightened.

"Hey," a voice called from behind the General. "Leave her alone!"

She looked over the General's shoulder and saw a man standing on the curb behind Abraxas. He wore a White Halls College football jacket, which he filled out with his large physique. Under normal circumstances, he would have been a great champion to come to her aid. Unfortunately, this wasn't a normal situation. He was in grave danger from the General and didn't even know it. His attempt to be a knight in shining armor could easily cost him his life.

General Abraxas released her arm and turned toward the stranger. As he smiled, the football player backed away from his pointed teeth.

"Say it again," the General hissed through his clenched teeth. Behind his back, a ball of flame began to form in his hand.

"Leave her alone," the man repeated with significantly less bravado.

"Oh, I will. I've found a much better plaything now."

The General whipped his hand around from his back. The ball of flame gripped in his palm burned a blindingly vibrant yellow. He reared back to throw the fireball at the young footballer.

Sammy lunged forward and struck the General's wrist as the older Fire Warrior was preparing to release. The flying ball went askew as it flew, narrowly avoiding the brave stranger. Instead of burning the young man where he stood, the ball of flame crashed through the pane of glass beside him before exploding against the interior display wall. The windows all along the storefront exploded outward in a shower of broken glass and roaring flames.

The football player threw up his hands defensively as the glass poured over him. As quickly as it had begun, the sudden burst of flames died away and the glass fell to the ground in a glistening rain.

The young man looked up with bewilderment. His feet seemed affixed to the ground as he stared at the homicidal Fire Warrior.

"Run!" Sammy yelled.

Her words cut through his stupor and he turned and ran. His sneakered feet crunched the glass underneath as he quickly disappeared around a corner.

Sammy stared toward the man as he retreated but her mind was swirling with confusion. She didn't know why she just saved that man's life. She didn't know him; hadn't seen him before just now. Instinctually, she knew that the Fire Warriors were going to burn away humanity so that the Earth could begin anew. Yet when faced with taking the life of a single human stranger, she couldn't bring herself to do it. It was a mirror to her experience with Xander when they were alone in the abandoned house. Something within her overrode her common sense and upbringing.

The General spun on Sammy angrily. Reaching out, he grabbed her wrists painfully, squeezing until she swore the bones underneath her skin would break. She whimpered in pain but refrained from crying out again.

"No more games, you stupid girl! Tell me where he lived!"

Sammy shook her head softly. Despite knowing he wouldn't think twice before killing her, she was beginning to accept that she couldn't betray the Wind Warriors to such a megalomaniac.

The heat on her wrists increased until she could hear the sizzling of her flesh underneath. She groaned loudly and her knees grew weak. The General leaned forward, his eyes smoldering with hatred.

Just when she didn't think she could take any more, she felt an invisible tugging on her gut. Like the butterfly feeling from before, this feeling was quite a bit stronger.

The General felt it too and quickly let her go. Sammy fell to the ground and curled into a ball, cradling her burned wrists against her chest. She knew the skin would heal; she always healed quickly from burns.

"He knows we're here," the General said. "I guess I won't need you to lead the way to them after all."

Reaching down, the General pulled her to her feet and shoved her ahead of him as they marched toward Xander's house.

The street was quiet as the pair walked down the

sidewalk. The air was filled with the lingering smell of soot and ash, a remnant of Xander and his grandfather's battle against the Fire Warriors in the nearby park.

Though the feeling in their gut was gone, the Wind Warrior's actions had done their damage. General Abraxas had been able to narrow down the location of Xander's house by following the elemental power. Standing now on the same street as the young Wind Warrior's home, the sly smile returned to the General's face.

"I know you're here," Abraxas yelled into the cool air. "Come and face me, Wind Warrior. Come and meet your doom."

Sammy held her breath, hoping the unseen Wind Warrior wouldn't be foolish enough to show himself against such a powerful Fire Warrior. She wanted to wave him away; to warn him about the danger. Unfortunately, General Abraxas had seen fit to tie her wrists with a leather cord, the other end of which was attached to his belt. He had given her just enough length on the leather rope to walk ahead of him but not enough to raise her hands above her head.

"You're a coward, like all the rest of your kind!" he yelled. "What is your plan? Stay out of sight until I leave? Rush off to warn the others? Your plan won't work because I'm not leaving!"

General Abraxas drew back his hand and flames enveloped his arm. The flames flickered and swirled as he formed them into a stream. The jet of flame leapt from his hand and struck a parked car nearby. The glass windshield shattered as the interior of the car burst into flames. Fire rolled out the broken side windows, spilling putrid black smoke into the air.

"Take a good look, Wind Warrior! I'll burn this entire street to the ground if you don't come out and face me. I'll kill every innocent person in this town until I flush you out! I'll…"

He stopped in mid-sentence as a biting sensation spread in his gut. A man leapt nimbly from a tree in front of a two-story house. The rosy-cheeked man glided fluidly through the air before touching down lithely in front of Abraxas. A cyclone of wind struck the General in the chest, lifting the surprised man from his feet. The leather cord jerked on Sammy's hands and she found herself jerked from her feet as Abraxas flew backward.

Before the Fire Warriors even hit the ground, the man had launched back into the air and disappeared into the nearby trees.

The General stood angrily and yanked Sammy back to her feet.

"Is this how you fight?" the General yelled. "You're only delaying the inevitable!"

A rustle of leaves warned the General seconds before a second cyclone struck him in the back, knocking him face first into the concrete. Sammy was jerked forward but managed to keep her feet. She dropped to a knee as the leather bit into her wrists. Slamming his fist into the ground, Abraxas raised his head just in time to see the Wind Warrior disappear once again into the tree line.

"Coward!"

General Abraxas climbed back to his feet hastily

and extended his hands toward the nearby trees. Flames leapt from his hands, igniting the leaf-laden branches. The vibrant green leaves curled and blackened quickly in the heat. The still-living wood sent pillars of white smoke into the air as the trees caught fire.

Turning, the General set tree after tree on fire. As he reached the end of the row of trees, the Wind Warrior emerged from the tree canopy. In his hand, the air shimmered as he prepared another air onslaught. Having prepared for the attack this time, the General held his ground and merely smiled at the confident Wind Warrior.

The floating Wind Warrior coalesced another miniature tornado in his hand and launched it at Abraxas. The General threw his arms out wide and let the cyclone hit him full force in the chest. Rather than staggering or falling like he had done before, General Abraxas absorbed the swirling air into his body.

The flames enveloping his arms burned even brighter as they were fed by the wind.

"Wind feeds the flame, or have you forgotten?" Abraxas laughed.

The Wind Warrior's eyes widened in surprise and he turned to flee.

Abraxas summoned dozens of small flaming orbs around his arms. He launched them in rapid succession toward the fleeing man. The Wind Warrior danced nimbly through the air, avoiding shot after shot. As he touched down on the ground and prepared to launch skyward once again, his foot slid momentarily in the muddy earth. The pause was brief but more than enough time for General Abraxas.

A pair of flaming orbs shot out at blinding speeds. They struck the Wind Warrior along his ribs, burning quickly through the man's thin shirt and scorching the skin beneath.

Sammy could smell the burned flesh from where she stood and her stomach soured. Despite her hands being bound, she managed to turn away so she wouldn't have to look.

The Wind Warrior dropped his arm to his side, protecting his wounded and exposed skin. On unsteady legs, he pushed off and flew straight upward.

General Abraxas followed his ascent but dismissed the flame orbs rather than throw them at the retreating figure.

"That's right," Abraxas muttered to himself. "Run home. Warn the others that I'm coming for you all."

The General's gaze dropped from the Wind Warrior and he scanned the houses nearby. Despite the supernatural battle that took place on the public street, most of the homes were dark and their curtains drawn tight. As he turned toward the two-story house in front of which the Wind Warrior had been hiding, he saw a pair of figures silhouetted in the window, watching the battle transpire.

Abraxas smiled to himself. He knew it would take a special type of person to stand at the window and watch elemental wielders battle one another. The parental type, unless he was mistaken.

"You let him go?" Sammy said in surprise. "Why didn't you just kill him?"

"Bait, dear Lady Balor," he grinned in response.

"So that's what the Wind Warrior and I am to you?" she replied insulted. "Bait?"

The General turned away from the window and the couple drew the curtains. "You misunderstand, my Lady. You and the Wind Warrior are the hook."

He snarled wickedly as he pointed to Xander's house. "They are the bait."

CHAPTER 17

Patrick launched a ball of pressurized air at Xander. The younger man easily sidestepped and created a gust that sent the ball flying back at the Irishman. Patrick dove aside, narrowly avoiding being struck. As he tried to climb back to his feet, Xander slammed a downdraft on top of him, driving him onto the mosaic floor. Patrick groaned and managed to lift a hand just far enough to tap on the floor, ending the sparring match.

Xander released the driving wind and stepped back, his chest heaving with exertion. He was exhausted from day after day of training but he had never felt more alive. Everywhere he went, the wind whispered to him. He felt connected to every inch of the island.

The aunts and uncles clapped from the seats around the open courtyard.

"He's getting better," Alicia said.

"I taught him all he knows, you know," Giovanni added with a wink.

Thea guffawed. "Then it's your fault he still has so far to go."

Giovanni laughed heartily. "You know you are impressed, *principessa*. You do not have to be coy with

Giovanni."

Xander walked over, beaming with pride. Patrick walked up behind him and patted him firmly on the back. "You did good, lad."

"Did you see the match, Grandpa?" Xander asked as the elder man walked out of the central building.

"I saw the important part. I watched you beat up that poor old man."

Everyone laughed as Patrick's jaw dropped in mock indignation. "You know I'm not the only old man around here, right?"

His grandfather opened his mouth to respond but froze with his mouth partly agape. The others stopped laughing as well. Even Xander sensed it—a subtle shift in the drifting of the island. It was so subtle that its meaning would have normally been lost but those gathered in the courtyard knew its meaning all too well. Robert was warning them that someone was approaching the island!

The group scattered, taking refuge behind or inside the nearby buildings. Xander could sense the mixture of excitement and fear in the air. If the Fire Warriors had found them already, then this very well could be a fight for their very existence.

Behind him, Alicia drew the air to her like a vacuum, creating a small vortex around her body. Xander could hear the hum of building air pockets around the perimeter of the courtyard. They were going to be prepared for whatever was coming.

Nearly thirty feet up the wall of water, the swirling waterspout parted and a single, round-faced man emerged. His flight was unsteady and he dipped dangerously close to one of the red-roofed buildings. At the last possible moment, his angle changed and he shot upward again. Near the peak of his ascent, the man lost his concentration and plummeted back toward the island's surface.

Giovanni broke from his hiding spot and shot skyward, catching the man only a few feet before he struck the tiled mosaic floor. The Italian drifted to the floor with the man cradled in his arms.

The other aunts and uncles retreated from their cover and rushed to Giovanni's side as he touched down on solid ground. Xander saw his grandfather hurry over as well and followed the old man's lead.

The Wind Warriors formed a circle around the plump man. His full cheeks were rose colored from exposure to intense winds. He had clearly been flying at an incredible pace to reach the island as quickly as he had. It wasn't the man's labored breathing or wind-swept face that concerned Xander. The side of his shirt had been burnt black and the soft skin beneath was blistered and scorched.

"Give him some air," his grandfather demanded.

The aunts and uncles took a reserved step back but their worried expressions didn't leave his face.

"Who is that?" Xander asked as his heart sank in his chest. He knew only one other Wind Warrior existed that he hadn't met before but he had been on a special assignment, guarding Xander's parents. If he was here, and burnt as he was, it could only mean bad news for his family.

"Who is that?" he repeated when no one

responded.

"It is Bart," Giovanni answered, placing a comforting arm around Xander's shoulders. "It's your Uncle Bart."

Bart slowly opened his eyes and coughed hoarsely. Every breath seemed to cause pain through his body but he forced himself into a seated position. He looked up through red-rimmed eyes and stared at Xander's grandfather.

"I'm sorry," he said over and over again. "I'm sorry. I'm so sorry."

"You don't have to be sorry," his grandfather said. "Just tell me what happened."

Bart took a deep breath and grimaced. With a slow exhale, he continued. "I was watching your son and daughter-in-law when I was ambushed by a Fire Warrior. He was far stronger than anything I'd seen before. I tried to hold him off but he burned me right through my strongest defenses. I wanted to stay, I really did, but I couldn't."

Tears streaked down his face. "I couldn't fight him so I came here as quickly as I could to warn you."

Xander staggered before collapsing onto a marble bench. The Fire Warriors clearly knew where Xander and his grandfather lived. Without Bart to defend them, there was no telling what damage someone like that would do to his parents.

"You did the right thing, Bart," his grandfather said. "You wouldn't have done any good staying there getting yourself killed."

"I'm sorry," Bart muttered again.

Xander's sorrow turned to a burning anger. He pushed away from the bench and wiped the threatening tears from his eyes with the back of his sleeve.

"It's a trap," Thea said. "You know it is. There's no possible way that a Fire Warrior defeats Bart so handily and then lets him live. He wants to draw you out."

"Let him try," Xander said to the gathered warriors.

His grandfather frowned. "I know you're worried but Thea's right." He shook his head before Xander could reply. "But so are you. We can't leave your parents undefended. I'll go and check on them."

"I'm going too."

"Take a look at Bart. He is far stronger than you are and this Fire Warrior easily defeated him. We're not dealing with the cannon fodder you and I fought in the park. Whoever this man is, he's dangerous."

Xander stepped forward, clenching and unclenching his fists. "That's all the more reason why we should go with numbers on our side. They're my parents. You can't stop me from going."

"He's right," Giovanni said. "I am the fastest of the flyers, no? I will go with the boy. If there is danger, no one will get you to safety faster than me."

"I'm going too," Bart said, pushing himself up from the ground.

"You can barely walk, Bart," Thea said. "Don't fool yourself."

"Lay back down, sweetie," Alicia said, patting Bart on the shoulder.

"It's my fault his family's in trouble," Bart

bellowed, his voice suddenly strong. "This happened on my watch and I'm going to make it right. End of discussion."

"Then we all go," Patrick said. "The whole bloody lot of us."

"No," his grandfather said quickly. "No, Thea's right. This feels like a trap. If it is, I'd rather we not all be caught together. If something happens to us, we have to ensure some of the Wind Caste survives.

"You three will stay here on the island and protect Robert," he continued. "If the Fire Warriors are moving against us, they may know about the island as well. Stay alert."

His grandfather stepped away from the others and walked to Xander's side. "Whatever happens, whatever we find, promise me you'll stay alive."

"If something has happened to them," Xander said, "there won't be a single Fire Warrior strong enough to stand in my way."

They nodded to Giovanni, who created a strong gust of wind beneath their feet. The quartet lifted off the ground and launched into the air, passing smoothly through the wall of water and emerging out over the vast ocean. They accelerated faster and faster, quickly exceeding the speed he and his grandfather had flown on their way to the island.

The wind whipped in Xander's face, blowing his dark hair behind him and stinging his eyes. He narrowed his eyes and focused on the landmass quickly approaching. His family was in danger and he was coming to their rescue. He clenched his fist and prayed Giovanni could get them to White Halls before it was too late.

CHAPTER 18

A dark pallor of old smoke hung in the air, visible for miles away. The plume of black smoke no longer billowed from a burning fire but hung in the air as an artifact from one recently extinguished.

None of the four spoke as they skimmed over the rooftops of the houses in White Halls but they shared a sense of foreboding. Xander wanted to vomit. Despite telling himself that there was still hope, something deep in his mind knew the truth. His limbs felt heavy despite not exerting his own powers on the flight. Giovanni must have been exhausted from carrying the group over the thousands of miles but he still seemed determined as they rushed toward the smoke.

When they reached the road leading to Xander's parent's house, Giovanni glided down to the street. As soon as his feet touched the asphalt, Xander sprinted toward his house.

He could smell the stinging smoke long before he reached the house. The acrid smoke filled the street, burning his lungs as he ran. He didn't know if the tears streaking down his cheeks were from smoke irritation or fear.

He knew the others were following as quickly

as they could but Xander swiftly left them far behind. The asphalt at his feet became dark with water. Puddles pooled in the pockmarks in the road and flowed like a stream against the curbs on either side of the street. The fire trucks were long gone and their hoses retracted but Xander could still see the cover left off from the fire hydrant across the street from his parent's home.

Xander's foot caught on the asphalt and he sprawled onto the road. His hands and knees scraped across the ground and skinned away the flesh. He wanted to climb back to his feet but his body felt weak. Slowly, he lifted his head and looked at the house.

Bright yellow police tape cordoned off the house. The roof had collapsed from the heat. Charred support beams were all that remained—now exposed to the afternoon sun. The front porch he had sat on so many nights, talking with his parents or grandfather, was buried underneath rubble from the second floor. The house had been gutted by flames, leaving blackened, hollow eyes where windows once stood. Nothing survived the destruction.

Xander pushed himself to his feet before the others caught up to him and walked unsteadily toward the house. Reaching out, he grasped the police tape in both hands and tore it in half.

His tennis shoes sunk into the muddy ground that was still saturated from hundreds of gallons of water. Beneath the smell of charred wood and broiled paint, he could smell a faint underlying scent of sulfur. He had only smelled something that pungent once before, when Sammy had cornered him in the abandoned house.

Xander clutched his chest as a wave of anguish washed over him. The Fire Warriors had been here—this was their fault. The sulfur smell was their calling card, left there for the Wind Warriors to find.

"Hey, you can't be here," a police officer called out as he approached the house. "It's not safe."

Xander turned toward the officer and wiped away the tears with the back of his sleeve. Seeing the sorrow in his eyes, the police officer relaxed and dropped his hand from the pistol on his belt.

"Are you okay?" the officer asked as he stepped onto the sidewalk. "Did you know the family that lived here?"

"They're my parents," Xander replied, unwilling to use the past tense when talking about them despite his burgeoning fears. "Where are they? What happened?"

"Oh, son, I'm so sorry. I'm not sure I'm the right person to be talking to you about this."

"Please," he said, pleading. "Please tell me what happened."

The officer sighed. "A fire started in the kitchen. Both your parents were asleep upstairs."

Xander swallowed a threatening sob. From the corner of his eyes, he could see the other warriors approaching.

"What happened to them?" he said softly.

"There was a lot of smoke in the house. They… they never woke up. It was painless—they went in their sleep."

His knees grew weak and his grandfather materialized by his side. Xander's deep loss was reflected in his grandfather's face but the elder man kept a stoic visage in front of the police officer.

"I'm here," his grandfather whispered into his ear. "I'm here."

"I'm really sorry to be the one to tell you," the officer said as he removed his hat and ran a nervous hand over his scalp.

"Thank you, Officer," Giovanni said, shaking the man's hand. "We appreciate your help."

The officer nodded at the men before walking back to his patrol car. The engine roared as the officer turned the key.

Xander felt a chill wash over him as the engine rumbled to life. It felt like electricity pouring through the muddy ground under his feet, coursing up through his legs before spreading through his core. Goose bumps rose on his arms and the hairs on the back of his neck stood on end as though statically charged.

He had felt something similar once before, seconds before the Fire Warriors ambushed him and his grandfather on the park bench.

His grandfather clenched his arms around Xander tighter, holding him closer. "Not now. Not while the police officer is still here."

Xander's tears quickly dried while he glanced from side to side, scanning for the Fire Warrior. He could sense Bart's palpable fear, having faced this warrior before. The fear Xander thought he'd felt was gone, replaced instead by an overwhelming need for revenge.

The police car pulled away from the curb and rolled down the road. Giovanni waved politely with a smile painted on his face. As it turned at the end of the otherwise empty road, the Italian dropped his hand. His grandfather released Xander, who staggered away from the older man before finding his balance.

The trees around them bent as the wind kicked up furiously. Xander's hair blew first into his face before the wind shifted directions chaotically, knocking the loose strands of hair back over his forehead.

From the side of the house, a single figure emerged. General Abraxas' shaven head glistened in the afternoon sun. His dark tattoos traced patterns down his cheeks before disappearing beneath his thick armor and fur-lined cloak.

"So these are the mighty Wind Warriors?" the General mocked. "I'm not impressed."

"You did this," Xander growled. "You killed my parents. I'll kill you!"

The power washed over and through him, coalescing in his hand in an orb of maddeningly swirling air. The wind was raw and untamed. When it launched from his hand, it surged through the air with a primal force rather than the disciplined technique he'd been practicing. The orb rocketed across the front lawn, aimed directly at the warrior's chest.

Abraxas' arm ignited in flames as he laughed. With a wave of his hand, he batted the orb harmlessly aside.

"You can't hope to defeat me. Wind feeds the flames, or have you forgotten so soon?"

Xander closed his eyes and tears squeezed from the corners of his eyes. He heard a concerned yell behind him but he ignored their warnings. This Fire Warrior killed his parents for no other reason than to draw him out of hiding. That sort of senseless brutality deserved the punishment Xander had in mind.

The wind built around him in a swirling vortex. He could hear his grandfather yelling at him from a great distance away but the roar of the growing tornado made his words inaudible.

Chunks of grass and mud were pulled from the ground by the swirling winds. He heard the fabric of his shirt tear as the howling winds pulled at his body from all angles. With a cry of anguish, Xander drove the tornado forward.

General Abraxas stood his ground with a wicked smile that revealed his pointed teeth. He crossed his arms in front of his face and both burst into flames.

The tornado struck him with a deafening crash. Shingles from the house's ruined roof cascaded onto the yard. A support beam, weakened from the fire, cracked on the porch.

Exhausted, Xander dropped to his knees. The swirling grass and mud slowed until it seemed to freeze in the air. At once, the debris collapsed into the yard in large, dirty piles.

In the center of the chaos, General Abraxas laughed again. He lowered his arms and Xander realized the man was completely unscathed. He wanted to cry again. The Fire Warrior was taking everything he had and brushing it aside. Xander's hopes of vengeance for his family were growing further and further away.

He forced himself back to a standing position

and let the wind build around him again.

"Xander, don't," his grandfather said from behind him. "He's too strong."

"Listen to the old man, boy! There's nothing you can do to stop me."

"Then I'll die trying!" Xander yelled. He concentrated again and the winds grew stronger around him. The energy pulled at his very essence, drawing its strength from his core. It felt like he was draining his life to fuel another assault.

"I wouldn't do that, if I were you," the General said. "Not if you want to keep your girlfriend alive."

Xander froze. The winds still swirled around him but the power ebbed from him.

Abraxas reached around the corner of the house and his hand closed around someone concealed there. With a tug, he pulled Sammy to the front yard. Her hands were tied in front of her with a leather thong. The General had the other end tied to his belt, keeping her tethered to him. His hand was clamped firmly around the back of her neck and she whimpered as the General squeezed against her throat.

"It's a trick," Bart said. "She's a Fire Warrior too. He wouldn't harm her."

Xander looked at the stern reservation on the General's face and panned to the pained fear on Sammy's. He knew instantly that this wasn't a bluff. The General was more than willing to kill her as a way to the Wind Warriors.

"Don't hurt her," Xander said. The wind around him died away.

"Xander," his grandfather said harshly. "Don't be a fool. He'll kill you."

"Let her go," Xander said, ignoring the protests. "Let her go and you can have me."

"No," Sammy said sternly. The fear faded away on her face. "Your grandfather's right. He'll kill you."

"Shut up, girl," Abraxas hissed.

"I screwed up with you," she said. A small flame appeared in front of her bound hands, burning through the leather thong. "I know that. But I can't stop thinking about you and I won't let you throw your life away for me."

"I told you to…" the General began before Sammy drove her elbow into his gut.

He doubled over in pain but kept his grip on her neck. As he righted himself, he jerked his arm backward. Sammy was pulled from her feet and launched through the air. She slammed painfully into a tree and slid down to the ground.

From where he stood, Xander couldn't see her moving. His worry turned to a searing rage. His eyes turned white and the wind roared around him. The power came from somewhere beyond him, like he was tapping into the fundamental nature of the elemental power.

"Sammy!" he yelled.

"Enough of this!" Abraxas said.

He raised his hands and the ground around Xander erupted in a cyclone of flames. They built into a pillar, swirling madly around him. The heat was oppressive, stealing the very oxygen from the air. Xander's clothes smoked as they threatened to ignite.

A bullish figure broke through the side of the burning pillar and knocked Xander free of the flames. He and Bart both coughed as they collapsed onto the ground, their skin blackened from the soot.

Bart rolled off him as Xander climbed to his feet. His grandfather and Giovanni had already engaged the General. Giovanni flew by the Fire Warrior, buffeting him with gusts of wind. His grandfather shot wind at him like spears, trying to pierce through his thick armor.

The General brushed the assaults aside. As Giovanni passed by again, Abraxas' hand shot up and grabbed the Italian's shirt. He flung the Wind Warrior aside and Giovanni crashed into the ground before rolling out of sight around the side of the building.

Seeing Xander back on his feet, Abraxas turned his attention back to the young warrior. A flaming sphere grew in his hand, burning from blue to green to red to virtually white. When the orb was practically too bright to look at any longer, the General pulled back his arm to throw.

Something triggered deep inside Xander, something primal and powerful. The wind surged within him far stronger than he had felt before. It saturated his body with energy until he felt unable to contain its purity. His eyes flashed a blinding white as he lost himself in its enveloping embrace.

The General launched his flaming orb and the wind leapt from Xander's body in response. The two elemental forces collided with enough strength to shake the ground. Sparks mixed with driving wind, sending shards of flames in all directions—like a firework exploding between them.

With the fireball destroyed, the power withdrew from Xander, leaving him weakened. His breath was ragged and his limbs felt heavy. His head sagged toward his chest. With an effort, he looked up in time to see the General throw a second orb of flame.

Xander raised his hand to deflect it but lacked the energy. He could do nothing as it spiraled toward him.

Just before the flame struck him, Bart threw himself in between Xander and the assault. The orb struck him in the chest and he fell limply to the ground.

The ground beneath Xander's feet shook as an earthquake rocked White Halls. He dropped to his knee for support as the shaking threatened to knock him from his feet.

The house shook violently. Wood creaked and shattered. Broken glass rattled in the ruined home. With a thunderous crack, the foundation split and the house caved in on itself. Clouds of dust and debris spewed across the front yard, engulfing the warriors.

"No!" he heard his grandfather yell from somewhere in the concealing smoke.

A bright red beam filled the air, illuminating the dust like lightning within a cloud. A single scream split the air before falling silent.

Xander was overwhelmingly exhausted. He lacked the energy to push himself up from his knee. Bart lay on the ground in front of him, smoke still rising from the wound on his chest. He couldn't see any of the others, though he strained to find a silhouette through the choking dust.

"Grandpa!" he yelled before being overwhelmed with a coughing fit. "Giovanni!"

A figure stepped through the smoke. Xander looked up hopefully but his hopes were crushed as he saw the dark armor and tattooed face of General Abraxas.

"They won't answer your calls," he said. "No one's left to rescue you."

Xander was crestfallen. He rocked back on his knees until he sat on his feet. He placed his hands on his lap, knowing that he had nothing left that could harm the General.

"Get it over with," he muttered.

"With pleasure."

The General raised his hands and a swirling maelstrom of fire grew between his palms. The ball grew beyond the size of his hand, expanding until it was over a foot across. Xander could feel the intense heat and he flinched involuntarily away from the flames.

"Your time is over, Wind Warrior. Long live the flame."

"I couldn't have said it better myself," Sammy said from behind him.

She placed her outstretched hand on the back of his cloak and the garment caught fire. He spun around in a panic, trying to control the growing flames but Sammy wouldn't release the cloak. She slid her other hand to his pants leg and set it on fire as well.

General Abraxas screamed as the fire quickly spread across his pants and up into his armor. It spread unnaturally quick as Sammy fed the flames with her power. Her beautiful blue eyes turned vibrant red as she focused, pushing her body to its limit.

The General finally broke free from her grip as she grew dizzy from exertion. Fully engulfed in flames, he turned away from the warriors and fled into the woods.

Sammy dropped beside Xander and cradled his face in her hands. Her hands were painfully hot but he didn't push her away. Blood trickled from a gash at her hairline and a faint bruise was growing along her cheek.

"Xander, I'm so sorry," she sobbed. "I tried to stop him. I tried."

"I know," he said weakly. He slid his arms around her neck and pulled her into a tight embrace.

They held each other for a long moment until they both felt strong enough to stand again.

As they stood, tears filled Sammy's eyes. "Xander, I'm so sorry. I didn't…"

Her words were lost as he kissed her. He could feel the heat radiating from her body and could taste the saltiness of the tears on her lips. The tension fled from her as she melted into his arms. Sammy slid her arms around his neck as he cradled her close to him.

As their lips parted, Xander felt at least some of the weight of the last few days' events lifted from his shoulders.

Sammy rested her head on his chest and nuzzled under his chin. Glancing past her, Xander looked over at Bart, who hadn't moved since the attack. Reaching up softly, he pulled Sammy's hands free from his neck and walked over and knelt beside him. His hands shook as he reached out and put his fingers against Bart's wrist, searching for a pulse.

"Is he…?" she asked.

Xander shook his head sadly and gently placed Bart's hand over his chest. Though he was tired, Xander summoned a wind and blew away the rest of the clinging dust cloud that blanketed the area.

With the air clear, he saw Giovanni crouched over his grandfather. The Italian was shirtless and his long hair was coated with mud and dirt. As the wind cleared away the rest of the dust, Giovanni looked over and saw the younger warrior.

"Xander!" Giovanni said, relieved. "Hurry here!"

Xander rushed over and froze short of his grandfather. The old man's face was painted with anguish and sweat mixed with the tears in his eyes. Giovanni's shirt was draped over his grandfather but Xander could still see the burnt arm jutting from underneath. He feared to pull the shirt aside and see what other damage had been done.

"Grandfather," Xander whispered.

"Hush," his grandfather said. "Don't you worry about this. I'll be back on my feet in no time."

Xander smiled politely but didn't believe the elder man. "I'm sure you will."

"We Siroccos are stubborn."

"To a fault," Xander joked with a strained laugh.

"Is Bart…?"

Xander shook his head. His grandfather let out an exasperated sigh, closed his eyes, and fell silent. For a moment, Xander feared he was going to lose his grandfather as well.

His grandfather opened his eyes again and looked at Sammy standing by Xander's side. "Is this her? Is this the Fire Warrior that you won't stop talking about?"

Sammy blushed and Xander nodded. "This is Sammy."

His grandfather smiled. "She's just as beautiful as you described."

Sammy slid her hand into Xander's and he clenched it tightly, for fear of ever letting her go.

"We need to leave here," Giovanni offered. "People will be coming soon. We can't let them find us here."

"Can you carry my grandfather and... and Bart?" Xander asked, fearing that Giovanni was too exhausted to make the trip back.

"I will make it happen."

He turned toward Sammy and looked into her blue eyes. Reaching up, he brushed aside some of the blonde hair that had matted in the blood on her forehead.

"Come with us," he said. "I don't know what it'll mean for us. I don't know where we'll go or what we'll do but at least we'll be together."

"Yes! But you have to know they'll come for us," she said. "They won't stop coming for all of you."

"Then we'll face them together," he said, squeezing her hand.

She slipped her hands around his neck and he created a buffer of wind beneath them. Giovanni cradled his grandfather carefully in his arms before pushing off from the ground and joining the other two in the air. Bart's body floated gently behind him, wrapped lovingly in the wind that held Giovanni aloft. As a family, they flew back to the island.

EPILOGUE

The Fire Warriors walked through the dense undergrowth of the woods, pushing aside clinging tree limbs. The trail of burnt ground and foliage was obvious as it cut a swath through the forest.

Leaves were curled aside from the heat. Limbs were blackened overhead and embers on the ground still smoldered red hot beneath their quickly cooling white exteriors. The woods were silent as all the animals had fled ahead of the fire.

The warriors crested a shallow ridge and found the valley consumed in thick, black smoke. They slid nimbly down the muddy slope on the back side of the ridge and entered the heart of the small forest fire.

The flames burned in a ring, consuming brush and tree bark in waves of crackling fire. In the wake of the flames, the ground was charred black. The warrior's boots shattered burnt plants as they stepped through the forest fire and into the soot-filled aftermath.

In the center of the burning ring, a man lay prostrate, his face buried in the ash. More soot and ash filled the air around him, settling over his naked form.

The closest Fire Warrior removed his cloak and placed it carefully over the burnt man, concealing the twisted and scorched skin underneath. At the touch of the cloak, the man stirred and opened an eye.

Slowly, the man pushed off the ground until he was standing on mangled legs. He looked up at the evening's sky through his one good eye. He huffed at the stars that were emerging as dusk settled over the valley.

"General Abraxas," the Fire Warrior said.

"Did you follow them?" Abraxas said through lips that had partially fused together in the flames. "Did you find them?"

"We lost them when they flew out over the ocean."

"But?" the General said dangerously.

"But the fishermen around the shore remarked that there has been strange weather far out in the ocean. We'll find them there, I'm sure of it."

"You had better be," Abraxas said. "Your life depends on it."

He closed his hand into a tense fist. "We'll find them, then I'll have my revenge!"

ACKNOWLEDGMENTS

The people that helped me put this book together are practically too numerous to mention. A tip of my hat goes to Josh, who will always hold the title of "my first fan". He, Amanda, Matt, and Justin read my works when I was nothing more than a hobbyist and have stuck with me ever since.

More recently, heartfelt gratitude has to go out to my amazing editor, Cynthia Shepp. Without you, I'd still be using, what I would consider, to be far, too, many, commas.

I think the greatest amount of gratitude has to be extended to the amazing ladies that run Clean Teen Publishing: Rebecca, Courtney, Dyan, and Marya. This book was only written on a whim as part of one of their anthology competitions. They read my novella and saw the potential for a true series. They were willing to take a risk on me and I can only hope I can repay their kindness. And from the marketing, web design, advertising, and cover artwork, they've been nothing less than amazing.

Finally, I wanted to say thank you to all my fellow indie authors, of which you really ARE too numerous to name. They've listened to my story lines and helped me work through troubling story arcs. They've cheered my successes when so many others were willing to put down my accomplishments. I can only hope I can stand by each of their sides as they cheer their own successes.

ABOUT THE AUTHOR

Jon Messenger, born 1979 in London, England, serves as a United States Army Major in the Medical Service Corps. Since graduating from the University of Southern California in 2002, writing Science Fiction has remained his passion, a passion that has continued through two deployments to Iraq and a humanitarian relief mission to Haiti. Jon wrote the "Brink of Distinction" trilogy, of which "Burden of Sisyphus" is the first book, while serving a 16-month deployment in Baghdad, Iraq. Visit Jon on his website at www.JonMessengerAuthor.com .

Clean Teen Publishing

CPSIA information can be obtained at www.ICGtesting.com
Printed in the USA
LVOW08s0041040616

491101LV00001B/4/P